As Blood Rages

Book 2 Macedo Ink Series

Bitten Twice

ISBN-13: 978-0-9839569-1-4

ALSO BY BITTEN TWICE

Macedo Ink Series:

Book One: A Blood Moon

Book Two: As Blood Rages

Book Three: For Blood Money (pending publication)

****

Marked

****

Free reading via author's website:

The Nodachi Line

WHAT OTHERS ARE SAYING ABOUT THE MACEDO INK SERIES

A Blood Moon "…it has a different twist to your usual vampire story."

"Series may leave you hungry for more…"

A Blood Moon "A fantastic, thrilling creative piece of work…"

Check out the reviews on Goodreads, Shelfari, Amazon, Barnes & Noble for more.

A FIVE STAR REVIEW FOR

AS BLOOD RAGES

As Blood Rages is book two in the Macedo Ink Series. It seems like I just finished with the first one, anticipating the second one with baited breath because I could not wait to see where Bitten took the characters. I loved the first one because I felt like I was in the story itself, experiencing the same things they were. This impressed me immensely, and showed me the talent, imagination and brilliance of this author. She makes sure her work keeps the attention of the reader, so much so, it had me sitting on the edge of my seat and very hard to put down in order to get some rest!

As Blood Rages flows where Blood Moon left off, I am excited to see if there is going to be a third book?! Once again the love and passion runs deep and makes a great companion when all is quiet in the house and are cuddled up under the blankets in my bed. Each time I read a book with an author's interpretation of a male vampire, I find myself falling in love with the character or man behind the words...and Alexander is no different. Love stories involving the vampire can ,and usually are very intense and erotic. It allows me to be taken away into my imagination, shutting out the rest of the world....away from the problems life has to offer...into a world filled with mystery, suspense, love, anger, bitterness, passion, all the great things that make up a wonderful tale. But as the last chapter appears and I come to the final word of the book, I feel disappointed...........but only until I pick up the next one! *smile*

I did not give a lot away about Bitten's newest baby, "As Blood Rages" because I want you to be as spellbound and excited about the book as I was and am! Bitten Twice has never let me down on any work she has written, and As Blood Rages is no different. I HIGHLY recommend this book to not all paranormal/vampire lovers out there, but those of you who love a great suspenseful, intense love story as well.

I give As Blood Rages five stars

Reviewed by Nora Chipley Barteau

http://norachipleybarteau.blogspot.com/

As Blood Rages

CONTENTS

As Blood Rages

ACKNOWLEDGMENTS

So many thanks go out to my family who have supported
me, my dogs who continue to be an awesome source of
inspiration, and those who love to laugh – you are great
motivation.

This book is dedicated to those who have stood by my side
through thick and thin. I know I don't have to drop names
because you all know who you are.

Always being there for me means so much more than the
words

"I Love you"

and yet that is exactly what it means.

Ditto.

Bitten Twice

PREFACE

The sheer chiffon curtains that habitually billowed in the gentle breezes, like the tails on a swallow-tailed humming-bird, were still. The scent of sweat-infused oil hung thick in the air. Alexander the Great, King of Macedonia sat in his usual place, his eyebrows knitted in concentration as he watched two men wrestling.

Fingers dimpled the well-oiled skin in an attempt to gain an indemnifying hold. Muscles bunched and strained against the opposing power of the other in a battle of strength and strategy.

Alexander's eyes followed a bead of sweat trailing down one of the wrestler's back. It grew in size as it collided with more moisture then traced a smooth path evading patches of skin laden with sand aided by gravitational pull, as his opponent showed his dominance. Alexander's focus was so intense he was oblivious to the whispers of the servants and the heavy footfalls of approaching man.

The wrestler slammed the other into the sand squashing the bead of sweat, and breaking Alexander's attention.

"Alexander," Black Cleitus called.

Black Cleitus was titled so, not for the color of his skin, for in truth, he was paler than Alexander. The title was a reflection of his military status.

Alexander turned with speed to mask the fact that the intrusion had caught him unaware. "Black Cleitus, what say you?" A smile graced his face, welcoming his friend and trusted companion.

"I've been looking for you."

"And now you have found me," Alexander grasped the forearm of his comrade in arms.

"The celebration will be starting shortly in the pavilion. The women, I hear, are beautiful. Will you be joining us?"

"I will, just as soon as this match has finished."

"Ah, you would rather watch oily naked men than dance with oily naked beautiful women?"

Alexander eyed him warily. Sensing no malice, his smile widened. He ignored the hushed gasps echoing along the walls, rose from his chair and said, "Cleitus, my good man."

Though Cleitus was a good head taller, he turned him to face the wrestling men. Pointing a finger, he continued, "Watch the darker skinned one. He has made the same maneuver three times and successfully turned the other who is lacking form. They seem to be of equal strength. The problem is that he has not figured out how to counter the other's measure." Alexander looked up at Black Cleitus, who knitted his brows as if trying to follow the thought process.

"This feels more like work than pleasure. Watching men's fruit get tossed is at the bottom of my list right now, sire."

"Cleitus, you watch the wrong end and you are missing the point my good friend." Alexander laughed.

"Knowing that there are beautiful women that may require my protection causes me to take leave," Black Cleitus said, as he retreated, "unless, of course, you require my presence, sire"

"I do not. I am moments behind you."

Alexander returned to his seat and resumed watching the match. "Place your hand higher and plant your feet wider in an opposing stance," he called to the losing wrestler, who complied with his instruction. Satisfied that he had discerned the counter measure to the winner's tactic, he rose again.

CHAPTER ONE

Jack's muffled footsteps echoed as she climbed the dark stairway. The rich scent of fruits and the savory smell of a cornucopia of meats laced the air. Her hand found her stomach as it rumbled from hunger.

Dim lighting in the stairwell cast dancing shadows on the huge granite rocks that formed the passage way. Raucous laughter filtered through the opening at the top of the stairs. Jack pressed her back against the cool rock, unsure of what she would find around the corner. She breathed steadily to calm her heart rate, while habit left her feeling for her gun. Unarmed again! She clenched her teeth and fists. Determination carried her forward.

"Come on in," a voice boomed across the expansive chamber that the passageway opened onto.

Jack clenched her jaw. Managing a dry swallow, she pressed forward. Finding her resolve, she rounded the opening into the chamber.

A muscular man lay on a pale gilded chaise lounge surrounded by women feeding him grapes. In a neighboring chaise lounge, a slender, but muscular woman was in a similar disposition. Both of them were dressed in togas which mirrored the decorum of the chamber. Jack took in the vaulted ceiling and rich gilded tapestries as she moved towards them.

"You're late," the woman said. Turning to her partner, she added, "Dion, do you want to do the honors, or should I?"

"I was sent at the designated time," Jack responded to the woman. She presumed she was the Greek Goddess, Athena.

"I'll take her," the man mumbled over a mouthful of grapes. After washing them down with a mouthful of liquid from a gilded goblet, he waved the women away and eased himself up.

Jack watched the big, Greek God stride towards her. One of his burly forearms encircled her mid stride and with a single motion from his hand, he made the floor crumble into oblivion that he jumped into.

Jack screamed as she fell. More raucous laughter filled her head.

Opening her eyes, she presumed the god to be Dionysus. His strength radiated energy that rippled through her as she continued to fall. With each pulsating energy blast, she drew sharp breaths. Clouds flew by in swirling mists at breakneck speed.

Eventually, the ground appeared. Jack felt like a skydiver without a parachute. Her only faith was in the arms of the man she had never met. At that point, she prayed that he was a god.

"Oh shit!" she clutched at Dionysus which drew chuckles from him.

Before they touched the ground, Dionysus leveled out. Jack realized then that she wasn't falling. She was flying, and at that moment was breezing through a war zone.

Dust, gun powder, and the stench of human decay filled her throat and nasal cavity leaving her winded. Bombs rained from black clouds, and flashes of shrapnel scattered like water fountain spray. Her hands flew up to defend her face against the flying debris. Yet, for all the horror, there was something that forced her to watch. Peeking through her fingers, she saw the destruction. People lay in twisted torturous pain, many with severed limbs waiting for the Angel of Death to rip their souls from their damaged shells. Unseeing eyes, fighting to function in ravaged bodies, were turned inside out; all reflections of the fragility of mortal life. Pain riddled the air. This death was living.

Jack choked on her emotions and the bile that threatened to spew. She was overcome by the sights war designed. Her eyes lingered on a little injured boy, who lay with his hands outstretched.

"Can he see me?" Jack whispered to Dionysus; her tongue felt thick.

"Not yet."

"I don't understand," Jack's voice trailed off as they disappeared into a crevice in the earth. "Is this hell?"

"Not yet. The balance has been lost and dark evil is claiming many lives. The Warriors of Light fight for them and we will persevere. Your purpose will be to restore the balance."

Dionysus' words left an imprint on Jack's mind as darkness enveloped her.

The thundering sound of tanks firing came to her ears, however the warzone was gone. The deep boom of what she had thought to be projectiles began to sound more like the bass of dance music. The rhythmic deep bass resonated like a heartbeat taking control of her own. She peered into the darkness. People were dancing. Not unlike a club in New York, the music was wild and alcohol flowed like water from a spring released dam. On occasion, she caught a red glimmer in the eyes of a man or woman partnered with a dancer. *Daemons!* She thought as she watched one, who was smiling, as he handed a human a drink. *They are preying on the innocent.*

Jack's eyes roved over the scene. The humans were oblivious. *Maybe too much drugs and alcohol numbed their senses.* Daemons were feeding and corrupting. This was indeed hell, and the first two levels seemed like a non-stop party. The tears were long gone.

Jack felt the pull of the music. She should forget about any responsibilities and just join the party. For Jack, losing control did not feel like fun at all though, but she could see the attraction.

Her eyes followed the multiple bite marks on the neck of a woman screaming with pleasure, as her daemon partner swung her around to the beat of the music. *Is she going to remember in the morning when reality awakens?*

The air thickened around Jack's throat as she descended further. Lack of oxygen made her head dizzy. As her eyes rolled over the fleeting scenery, she wondered how much longer she could hold on.

Dionysus stopped on the fifth level over Hell's Canyon. By then, Jack was almost delirious as her brain fought for oxygen. Her clothes felt restrictive. Her head languished as she strained to breathe and her hand feebly grasped her neck to release an invisible restraint. She stared at Dionysus wild eyed with fear. Jack realized that her struggles were futile. There was no way she could get out of hell alone with the few seconds she had left, and asking Dionysus to take her back seemed out of the question. He looked like he was ready to make a sacrifice of her to the river below. Jack allowed the drunken feeling to wash over her as her vision began to tunnel.

"Alex," she called his name in the barest of whispers.

"Jack," the voice sounded urgent.

Jack aka Jacqui Brunson, former private detective and newly appointed Peace Keeper was responsible for the balance between heaven and hell. She opened her eyes that connected with the titanium eyes of Alexander, a two thousand year old vampire; her protector, Dark Angel, and most trusted friend.

She took in a long breath of air, grasped her throat then ran her hands down her chest and along the bed feeling the dampened bed linens.

"Jack, you're okay. You're in bed." Alex leaned over her and placed a soothing hand on her forehead. "Maybe a bad dream," he said, as he examined the viscosity of her perspiration before rolling a diminishing bead of sweat between his thumb and forefinger.

"What happened to you?"

"What do you mean?" Alex cocked an eyebrow.

"You're all vamped out," Jack stared at his black leathery wings, fangs, and well-muscled chest.

"You called me. It sounded life-threatening. I came ready for battle." Alex stood up and snapped his wings gone. "I was in the middle of changing when I heard you." He normalized his fangs which made him look less intimidating. His tousled, dirty brown hair framed his face and his smile lit up his eyes. Sitting on the bed, he said, "So tell me, what did you dream about this time?"

Jack swung her legs off the bed in the opposite direction from him. Seeing him half naked always made her want to touch him. It was like window shopping without money. She often asked, *Why try it on when you know you can't afford it?*

"The little boy and the trip that went along with it," she looked over her shoulder at him shrugging her shoulders.

"So, you don't want to talk about it?" Alex smiled, "you know, the dreams will go in time."

"So they say." Jack inhaled sharply as Alex appeared in front of her. Closing her eyes, she steadied herself against her desire to give herself to him. "I'm good Alex. I'm going to get dressed and go to the kitchen to have breakfast. We can talk later about it all?"

Jack felt the barest of kisses on her forehead. She opened her eyes and he was gone, as unobtrusive as the change from night to day. Sighing with relief, she flopped into the closest armchair in her suite at Macedo Inc. and stared into the full length mirror opposite her. Aimlessly, she watched as the wolf tattoo ward made its way down her leg. She felt a slight tingling sensation as it moved. A smile came to her face, *I remember Sam putting you there.* The wolf stared back at her. *You have done a good job in protecting me so far, although sometimes I'm not always ready for you to be walking about.*

She guessed changes were happening to everyone. First, Sam was her assistant then she finds her witch-hood and becomes the owner of La Sangre de Vida, a private blood bank that hosted to hospitals and catered to the upper echelon of vampires. Jack twisted her body to see if she could see the panther, the second ward Sam placed somewhere on her back. They seemed to have free reign of her body so it was often hard to keep track of where they were until they moved. She caught sight of the Crest of Macedo at the nape of her neck, and the Aegis that was bestowed on her by Athena at the initiation and cleansing. After twisting positions, Jack spied the panther curled up between her shoulder blades.

"I'm a billboard," she laughed shaking her head. Sinking into the chair, she looked at her hands that showed two dark crosses marking her palms from where the Archangel Raphael had removed poison from her system. Her laughter faded.

She grabbed a pair of jeans and white t-shirt that was draped over the back of the armchair and headed into the shower. Although she knew the water couldn't wash any of it off, something about being in water always made her feel better.

CHAPTER TWO

The bell from the elevator sounded and the door opened.

Jack looked at the smiling expectant faces that greeted her from the kitchen. Since everyone had moved into the Macedo Tower, Alex remodeled the top floors as living quarters. Jack smiled as she remembered the talk he had with her; she was the only one who needed convincing. It was pretty clear that Lina would move in with him on the first floor since becoming husband and wife, or whatever vampires and daemons do.

Sam spent most of her time with Max in the penthouse suite, although she still kept her apartment uptown.

Jack smiled, being the Peace Keeper between the good, bad, and the balance definitely had come at a price, but living at the Macedo Tower wasn't all that bad.

"Hey Jack, you're up," Sam gushed, her curly hair escaping from the ponytail that she had fashioned. "Can I get you some coffee and pancakes? It's all fresh," she wriggled out the arms of her new boyfriend, Max, Alex's adopted human son, to get the coffee in anticipation of Jack's response.

"Yes, to the coffee, and maybe later to the pancakes." Jack was not accustomed to seeing so many people first thing in the morning. While her apartment had all the amenities and her own kitchen -- too lavish and stylish to be called efficiency -- there was something about the coffee maker in the community kitchen that called her like a zombie from its grave. "Can we dial the sun back just a little bit?"

Max walked to the wall; he punched in the code to access the ceiling to floor digital windows and increased the tint on them.

"Have a seat Jack, the pancakes were excellent, just in case later comes sooner," Lina moved a chair next to her.

Jack forced a smile. She was still unsure about Lina and her motives. She also happened to be the devil's daughter, who had been trapped in heaven; which turned out to be not such a great place for hell's spawn.

"I'm so not ready for food right now," she gave a thumb up to Max, satisfied that the room was no longer bright. She wondered why it affected her more than Lina.

"The dreams will change or disappear in time," Lina offered.

"Yeah, I keep hearing that." Jack accepted the coffee from Sam and sipped it, relishing the warmth and appreciating the immediate jolt from the caffeine. "What were you guys chatting about before I disrupted things?"

"Oh, I was telling Lina that you said you saw fayerie," Sam giggled.

"I was quite curious when Sam told me you and Alex encountered Fay warriors," Lina smiled, "Alex is not…"

Jack watched as she looked for a word.

"Alex is not partial to fay." Lina went on.

"Yes, I know." Jack couldn't help but chuckle over her coffee remembering an event.

"Where did you find them?" Lina turned to face her.

"They were guarding one of the portals to heaven," Jack questioned why she didn't know and was skeptical as to how much information she should divulge. Curiosity was written all over her face. Lina, like Alex, could read thoughts from anyone of her choosing. Was she being nice?

"Did he get all twitchy and fidgety?" she playfully motioned with her body, her heavy Spanish accent apparent.

"Yup! Just like that." Jack laughed as did Sam and Max at Lina's antics.

"So, what is fay exactly?" Max asked.

"Fay is like an overall category for the realm of magic. They have a light and a dark, as do we. Most people think of pixies and nymphs, or other winged creatures; the world of fay is much bigger than that. A fayerie is a fay magical creature, but the fayerie warriors don't like to be called fayeries, especially the males, because of the human connotation that it is a little light in the wing," Lina laughed, while flopping her hands around.

"Trust me; men are men no matter what species or realm they are from. It's like the one gene is consistent." Lina looked at Max and feigned her apology for including him. "I'm sorry honey."

Jack and Sam burst into laughter, as Max excused himself to answer a phone call.

"I guess we all have our issues," Lina smiled and sipped her cup of microwave warmed blood.

Jack stared at Lina, never having considered that she had issues. She found Lina's flat emotionless face cold and calculating. It put her on edge. "What kind of issues do you have?"

Lina leaned forward and whispered, "Well since we are sharing. I have been feeling rather confused since I have been there." Lina gestured upwards, as most devils and daemons did.

She still couldn't bring herself to speak openly about heaven; being the devil's daughter didn't lessen her caution.

"The only other time that I felt like that was when I bumped into Alejandro by the sea of Tiberias many years ago. We sat on a rock on the mountainside listening to his son." Lina pointed upwards again, her face softened at the onset of her memories.

"It was crazy; he was stuck in my head like a bad song. My father said that I had gone loopy. He grounded me on Sub-Seven until I was right in the head again. It was years until I could prove to him that I was still the same wicked little girl that he sired."

Jack opened her eyes wide. "You have seen Jesus?" she thought Lina looked back at her as if she was wearing a 'stupid' sign on her forehead.

"Haven't you been listening? I wasn't the only one. There were like five thousand other people there. I suppose if any of them were still alive I could get you another witness, other than Alejandro, of course."

"Wow! That's like right out of the Bible, except the Bible says there weren't any women there."

"Oh si, lo que sea… I was there. Do you think out of five thousand men that they were going to write about women? And when he drew on his father's power to magically multiply the food, who do you think served it? Men back then didn't lift a finger for themselves. Sabes!"

"That makes you how old?" Jack asked, staring at Lina's flawless skin that appeared ageless and not a day over twenty-five.

"I was old enough to make a man leave his new wife. I was old enough to start rifts between friends and wars between nations. But that really doesn't answer your question does it?" Lina appeared contemplative for a moment with her finger poised pulling on her bottom lip; she then laughed looking at Jack who was mortified.

Undaunted, Lina went on, "I suppose the right thing to say, or the more human thing to say would be, I don't recall. Only mortals count in numbers, honey. Immortals remember events and eras, not minutes, days, and hours. And stop looking at me like that. That look is not necessarily attractive."

Jack laughed, as Lina mimicked her. "I'm sorry. It's just that sometimes I forget that you're not the girl next door."

Lina joined her laughter and Jack wondered how many possessions she had done of various girls next door.

"How do you know that the girl next door isn't worse?"

"Good point." Jack said, still laughing.

CHAPTER THREE

Alex closed his connection with the Vampire Nation and stared at the spinning Macedo logo on the monitors. The Gryphon that sat on the crest with his name written in ancient Greek letters seemed to stare at him, as the crest spun about in a three hundred and sixty degree pivot. His mind almost drifted into muddled thoughts until the impression of warm vanilla permeated the room.

"Good evening, Miguel. Are you going to hang around all night, or did you want to talk? You know shiftiness is not one of your best angelic attributes."

"Are you experiencing problems in paradise, Alexander?"

Miguel, Jack's appointed Warrior of Light and Archangel of the Heavens, popped in without materializing during the last few minutes of Alex's meeting with the Vampire Council. Alex wondered if he had been sent to eavesdrop. He was sure he was there for a few minutes; that was all he needed, since the Lord Chancellor gave a summary of the discussion.

Alex knew that Miguel was now aware that the Council had rejected his choices for control of the Russian lands, but had allowed him time to make another selection. Miguel would also know that the Vampiric Council were questioning Alex's abilities to maintain the status of a Dark Guardian, as well as maintaining the responsibilities of managing his territory and seat as an Ancient on the Vampire Council. If the angel were not an advocate of Light, he would be more worried; still, he wondered if Miguel could be turned. If so, Miguel would not be the first angel to have fallen. He growled and muttered some obscenity in vampiric tongue.

"So, do you come bearing good news, angel, or are you a messenger of doom, eavesdropping like a carrier pigeon?"

Alex watched the scowl cover Miguel's face like the shadow from a pending rainstorm. He could see that he had hit a sore spot. Miguel clearly resented being considered a messenger of doom. Although angels were considered messengers, Miguel considered himself a warrior and was always ready to fight.

"I do not bring good news; if this is not a good time I can wait, as you will find out soon enough." Miguel gritted his teeth.

Alex sat straight up in his chair. "Why would you share information with me?"

"When you fought for Lina against Hell's Fifth Level daemon, Xylar, you did not use dark power to win." Miguel stared at him.

Alex sat back in the chair. Was the angel sizing him? He remembered the instant fury that monopolized and coursed throughout him when Lina was ported by Xylar, the daemon, who marked Jack for a daemon's bride, and the same daemon who targeted Lina for expiration. In both cases, Alex thwarted his plan. He remembered the lack of release when Xylar expired.

He looked up at Miguel, confused.

"You didn't even realize, did you?" Miguel laughed throwing his head back.

19

"You seem pleased with yourself," Alex growled waiting for all to come clear.

Miguel sat in a chair in front of Alex's desk. "The power that surged within you came from pure love for your devil. That is the intensity that people feel when they truly love each other; a mother, for a son, a father, for a daughter, or a man for his woman."

"What does this have to do with the information you have." Alex had already determined that he loved Lina on his own; having Miguel derive the same was of no consequence to him. He also knew that no matter what love he had for Lina, it could never compare to the love held dormant in his heart for Jack. A love always cherished; never allowed to blossom.

Alex guarded his thoughts while he ruminated upon the women in his life, wondering what the archangel could possibly have to offer him, of all people.

"There will be a trial," Miguel answered warily.

Alex was known for his temper, and although many years had dampened the fuse, for many, he was still considered a wildcard.

"Who will be on trial?"

"You and your devil."

Alex jumped to his feet. "Angel, do not toy with me. What games are being played? We have committed no crime."

Miguel gave him a cold stare as if waiting for something. Alex took a deep breath allowing his temper to subside.

"Please continue," he motioned to Miguel and sat back in chair watching the angel size him up. Feeling the familiar rise of anger stir in his gut, he smiled trying to exude a cool façade of calm.

"There are those that are not certain that you should be the Dark Warrior." Miguel shifted in his chair. "Even if you are able to maintain that role; there are those that would prefer that you couldn't." Miguel cocked his head before continuing. "Some believe that you have too much influence here in Terra with your recent acquisition of Russia. You are able to enter heaven and come out unscathed. No Dark Angel has ever been able to do that. In addition you currently outrank me, which lends to the belief that there is an imbalance in favor of Darkness that may have undue influence on the Keeper. That, coupled with the dark power that Dionysus may have bestowed on the Peace Keeper, leads us all to pray that Athena saw fit to grant her the gift of wisdom to balance the dark power that surrounds her."

"Who else would be the candidate?" Alex asked, mentally preparing for another fight while thinking of his expectant wife and unborn. He was well aware that the candidate would be expected to fight a death match for the privilege of guarding the Peace Keeper.

"Your devil."

"She no longer fills the requirements, and she is breeding," Alex growled, observing Miguel as he rose from the chair and gave him a rare, genuine smile, which emanated warmth. "Why do you volunteer this information?"

"I am only considering Jack's safety, Nightwalker."

"How so Angel? I ensure that I protect my women."

"But should you be put in a position to choose, which one will you protect…?" Miguel left his question hanging.

Alex stood, fighting to squelch the anger that boiled within him. His eyes burned white, as the need to protect his family dominated his thoughts. The lights flickered in his office. He summoned the resolve for control.

"You have become a very curious creature of the night, Alexander, very curious." Miguel's voice became an impression as he dematerialized.

Alex growled, trying to shake off his anger.

"They have the same effect on me."

Alex spun around to find Lucifer sitting on the leather sofa in the sunken living room, adjacent to his office. He noticed that the stark contrast of the dark mahogany leather, against the pale ivory of the white suit that Lucifer wore. It made him look old and frail.

"To what do I owe this honor?" Alex stepped down from his office with a broad smile. *I will not underestimate him. This is just another mental ploy to get me to drop my guard.*

"There is a small business matter that I would like to discuss with you." Lucifer reciprocated the smile.

Alex positioned himself across from the fallen angel, easing onto the leather couch. He never let his eyes leave Lucifer's face for a moment. "And what matter would that be, sir?"

"My daughter."

Alex leaned forward, his muscles tensed. He was unsure how a battle with the greatest underlord of hell might end up; he wanted to be prepared. "Is something amiss with our affairs below? I admit that I have not been as involved as I could be..." Alex let his voice trail as he calculated Lucifer's response.

"Your affairs are the least of my concerns at this point." Lucifer leaned forward and adjusted his suit jacket before continuing. "It would appear that there will be a trial that may open a position for my daughter, either as the Dark Angel, or as the Peace Keeper."

Alex felt the weight of Lucifer's gaze upon him. He controlled his response, as he likened the gaze to the doors sealing an Egyptian tomb; heavy and one miscalculated move could seal the eternal fate for Jack, Lina, and himself. "The Angel did share that there would be a trial." Alex crossed his legs. "Tell me more about the opportunity?"

"I share much with you." Lucifer smiled.

"I ask only to be prepared to best serve all of our needs." Alex returned the smile, maintaining his control. The mindless banter, while it had purpose, was more about dominance and control than it ever could be about direction.

"Perhaps you have all you need to watch for the opportunity, son," Lucifer dematerialized.

Alex exhaled as he watched the impression on the leather couch disappear. The only imprint of Lucifer's visit was now just one stamped in his memory. He got up and smoothed the leather on the couch where the Underlord had sat more in an attempt to settle his anger than to smooth the nonexistent wrinkle in the fabric.

I wonder what the sneaky old dog has up his sleeve. Clearly, either Jack or Lina are going to be in danger. What does the Council believe a trial will resolve? Lina is in no position to be battling, or defending a position. She shouldn't even be shifting. What are they all thinking?

Alex vamped out and begun pacing with one arm folded across his chest while the other took the weight of his chin. He snapped his wings closed when he sensed Lina coming down the hallway. *She need not know of the visits as of yet. They will only cause worry.*

Halfway to the office doors, Alex smelled the familiar vanilla scent of Miguel waft into his nostrils again.

****

Lina looked up to find Miguel standing in front of her. "Diablo, you startled me," her Spanish accent was thick.

"Me?" Miguel smiled, "how could I ever startle you? Are you losing some of your senses carrying these little ones?"

Lina looked at Miguel; his smile was kind and welcoming. The realization hit her that she should have known he was there long before he had finished arriving. Her eyes narrowed. She wondered what he would do with the knowledge of her vulnerability.

Miguel put his hands up. "I mean no harm by acknowledging your difficulties. I only mean to offer a suggestion."

"Which is?" Lina was suspicious.

"I believe that you are suffering from deficiencies. While the bottled blood that you are drinking is sustaining you, I don't believe that it is getting all the needed nutrients to the little ones. I think that you need fresh blood."

Lina laughed, "And you, of all beings, are suggesting that I prey on people to satisfy the needs of my offspring?"

"No, not at all, I am suggesting that you take your favorite form as a lioness and hunt on the plains, perhaps. That blood should sustain all of you."

Lina cocked her head acknowledging that she did feel wearier, and required blood with greater frequency. "Why would a Warrior of the Light help a Son of Darkness?"

Miguel lowered his voice. "I have watched you, Prince of Abaddon, and find that you have helped the Peace Keeper on more than one occasion. For this reason I help you now."

Lina raised her eyebrows. "You know that I cannot initiate the travel."

"I do."

"So, you are proposing to carry me?"

"Do you accept?" Miguel raised his eyebrows and cracked his typically stony facade with a smile, as he extended his arm towards Lina.

Lina's mind raced over the pros and cons. Her eyes flickered down the hallway where the closed doors of the apartment she now shared with Alex stood; just beyond her natural eyesight. Pursing her lips, she reached out and stepped with caution into Miguel's awaiting embrace. "I do," Lina looked down placing her hands on her round belly, "under one condition."

Miguel's smile faded. "Name it and I will let you know if I am able to comply."

Lina looked down the hallway one last time before shaking her index finger at him, "Speak of this to no one, or I will personally stake you to the rocks on the mountainside of the River Styx so the harpies may eternally pick the flesh from your bones."

"Not even Alex?"

"Most of all, not Alex," Lina narrowed her eyes glaring at Miguel, thinking that everything with Alex had been so complicated lately.

"I will ignore the threat and I will maintain the secrecy you desire."

Satisfied, Lina stepped in Miguel's arms and they disappeared from the hallway in a rush of air.

CHAPTER FOUR

Alex opened his office door and stepped out into the hallway. He fully expected to find Miguel and Lina there. The empty hallway greeted him. His brows furrowed, from the entanglement of their scents. He made a mental note to ask them separately about the growing number of instances he found their scents intertwined. In disgust, he headed towards the elevator. He exhaled when he passed the point in the hallway where their scents were strongest, dust particles fell around him. *They just left. Miguel must have taken her, because she cannot travel. That meant Lina consented to him carrying her. Most curious.*

Leaning against the wall of the elevator bank, he passed the time listening to the varying thoughts that drifted his way. He tried to stay away from the possibilities that Lina had opted for the angel over him. A familiar voice interrupted him.

"I suppose even the head of the company has to wait for the elevator?"

Alex turned to find himself face-to-face with Ishtyn of Cairn, Senior Councilman of the Vampire Council and Magistrate of the Global Magical Association. Smiling, he extended his hand to grasp the pale forearm of the other in greeting. "To what do I owe this honor?"

"Can we go somewhere and talk. This traveling has made me a bit weary." Ishtyn returned the grip with an equal smile.

"Of course, let's head to my office." Alex headed back down the hallway, wondering what the ancient vampire would have to say. The news had to be important enough for him to travel during the day, especially as Council had so many issues with him and his circumstances. "Can I get you something to drink? I'm sure this isn't a casual visit?"

"Always so astute Alexander." A pulsating blue vein stood out against the flame red of Ishtyn's hair. "Yes, a drink would be quite nice."

Opening the door to his office, Alex used his preternatural speed to lock the office door. Locating two glasses and a bottle of blood, he positioned himself on the couch opposite Ishtyn. A casual air masked his anticipation as he poured some La Sangre de Vida. He passed Ishtyn the stem less crystal glass, finding it curious that the ancient vampire had sealed his mind to him blocking Alex from connecting mentally or reading his mind.

"There will be a trial at Peace Palace," Ishtyn swirled the dark liquid around the glass, as if at a wine tasting. "A?"

"AB actually, and I'm aware."

"Really? News travels fast."

"Yes, well you are my third Christmas ghost, although perhaps a tad out of order, but ne'er the less. You have some information to share?" Although Alex smiled, his eyes were calculating.

"Many believe that you are becoming too powerful…" Ishtyn left his words unfinished.

Alex watched the other vamp; experience told him that Ishtyn had not played all of his cards. He was comfortable with the silence that hung between them.

"You have real estate on terra and in the underworld. Many were not happy with the decision to allow you to select the vampire that controls Russia. Augustine, although a good choice, leaves others thinking that he is still within your control."

"He was released from my service."

"Understood, but perception is what it is."

"I helped you into your seat at the Council." Alex said, aware that he unnerved Ishtyn. He watched the recognition flicker across the vamp's face, the pulsating blue vein quickened at Ishtyn's temple. Alex scented a hint of moisture from the ancient's skin.

"There is that," Ishtyn uncrossed and crossed his legs adjusting his composure.

"What is being questioned here, my word? My honor? Need I defend both?" Alex maintained his cool exterior; inside, rage boiled.

"This…" Ishtyn let his words hang, "this is actually not about you."

"Then we have nothing to talk about," Alex lifted himself out of the couch.

"Walk with care old friend. Vampires are questioning your loyalty and ability to defend the Keeper." Ishtyn slowly rose to meet Alex's glare

"Ishtyn, I have managed my commitments for years without fail."

"Yes, but now there are many waiting for you to make a mistake, or effect one; the Keeper's life is too precious to wait for that to happen."

"Nothing is guaranteed, no matter who you have guarding the Keeper. I will manage my business as I always have and anything, or anyone that presents a threat." Alex's tone was cold and his intent was clear.

"Coming here is not without consequence," Ishtyn sighed.

"I value your friendship old friend. Your message is grim. I appreciate the risk that you have taken."

Alex lightened his mood to crack the barest of smiles, as he ushered Ishtyn out into the hallway.

CHAPTER FIVE

Jack watched Sam and Max as they sent each other longing looks and secret smiles. *I wonder if I could ever let myself trust someone completely. Well, I have trusted Alex with much, but it's not the same, I don't think. And Miguel, my frosty angel, he's just so hot and cold, I sometimes don't know if I'm coming or going. And much recently he's been doing more going.*

Jack sipped some coffee, glad that Lina had left to go and find Alex. *I don't know what her deal is. Or maybe I don't know what my deal is. I need to back off in that department. I know it. Lina*

33

is with Alex now; I just don't know why I still can't let go of... her thoughts were interrupted by the sound of the elevator's arrival.

Her face lit up as Alex came striding towards her. "Hey there," she blocked her mind as she stood to greet him, while she stuck her hands in her back jeans pockets attempting to portray an open character. "What are you doing here?"

Alex grinned at the question, "Have I been banned from my own kitchen?

"No. That's not what I mean." Jack said, visibly flustered. "Lina went to go find you. I guess I was just expecting that you'd be with her."

"I'm sorry to disappoint." Alex looked directly at her.

Jack couldn't help but stare into his titanium grey eyes. She wanted to reach out and smooth the curl in his eyebrows and feel the cool pressure of his lips. Her prior thoughts of holding back her desires against his charms were squelched.

"No. I don't mean it like that," she cocked her head, realizing that Alex was joking. "Alex, don't be difficult," she felt herself being coy and tapped him playfully on the arm; a reminder that they were just friends.

"Did you say Lina went to find me?" Alex asked.

Jack scanned his face; she could tell he was deep in thought. "Yes, that's what she said, is everything alright?"

She watched him nod a greeting to Sam and Max.

"I need to speak to you for a minute," his voice was hushed.

She watched him glance at Sam and Max again before returning his focus to her jade, green eyes. She slid off the high backed chair wondering if they were going to have a conversation about Lina, one she was sure that was long overdue. "Sure."

Jack allowed Alex to steer her towards the elevator. She could feel the slight pressure of his fingertips at the small of her back. The same hands she had watched savagely rip apart a daemon, impending threat, or rival, now gave the gentlest of caress and guidance. She stepped into the elevator.

"We need to go somewhere private."

"What's more private than an elevator for two?" Jack smiled at Sam and Max watching their faces until the doors blocked her view. "Where do you suggest?"

"Come."

Alex extended his hand. Jack knew the simple offer would only mean that they would teleport somewhere. She stepped towards him and felt his hand slide up her back until his palm rested casually against the nape of her neck. She felt his protective fingers cradling her head, as he pulled her into the firmness of his body. Shivers ran up her spine. Her body responded to his closeness. She couldn't deny her attraction; she wrapped her arms around him.

"Cold?"

"No." Jack mumbled burying her head in his chest. Alex was a good head taller than she was. The perfect height when he held her, unlike Miguel, whose frame was bulkier and taller than Alex's. Except that lately, Alex seemed to be around more frequently than Miguel.

"You ready?"

Jack didn't trust her voice. She nodded, tightening her arms around him and squeezing her eyes ready for him to snap his wings and catch a rift. When the rush of air stopped, Jack heard strange sounds. She opened her eyes looking up in question at Alex. "Where are we?"

"India, I just needed to talk to you alone. Things are going to get a little hairy around here and I need you to know that you can trust me." Alex snapped his wings gone and brushed a wisp of hair from Jack's forehead, tucking it behind her ear.

A slow smile crept across her face. "Alex, you know I trust you. What's going on?"

"I'm not sure yet. I just know that things may not appear as they are. I was visited by Miguel and then him."

Jack watched Alex point downwards with his finger, and she caught on that he was referencing Lucifer, Lina's father.

She remembered that calling his name could manufacture his presence. She nodded, urging Alex on with his story.

"Then Ishtyn stopped by with the same news. After, I caught Miguel and Lina's scents intertwined, like they were together."

"Together?" Jack raised her eyebrows remembering Miguel's distaste for Lina.

"Yes, in each other's arms type of together."

"Are you jealous?" Jack wondered if she also weren't feeling slightly miffed, she felt something stir in her stomach.

"I'm not sure what's going on; if there ever comes a time where the cards don't seem to be stacked right, know you can count on me to be there for you, no matter what. Three people bearing the same news in unsolicited visits can only be a bad omen."

"What did Miguel want?" Jack prompted, while wondering if the news would shed any light on his absence, or the mysterious partnership with Lina.

"He told me that there will be a trial held to determine who will be the Dark Angel."

Jack pursed her lips in thought. *If not Alex then Lina. Maybe Miguel's trying to get Alex out of the picture. Ugh! Or what if he and Lina were shacking up then I'd have the both of them over my shoulder – equally ugh.* "So, then what did he want?" Jack tried to refocus.

"He didn't really say. I'm sure there is some grand scheme afoot."

Jack narrowed her eyes, recognizing that Alex was being cautious with his answer. While he would want her to have as much information as possible, he would also want to be able to answer truthfully if he had to take a blood oath. Jack wondered what he was holding back. She opted not to press him.

"Are you worried about the trial?" she scanned his face hoping to find more answers. Instead, she found herself wanting Alex to touch her, just as the fog caressed the tops of the trees on the mountainside.

"I'm worried about you."

"Why?"

"I'm worried about your safety if I can't maintain the status quo."

"What could happen?"

"I don't want to speak it into a reality."

Jack offered no resistance when he pulled her into him. His hand found the nape of her neck leaving the other to rest at the small of her back. His fingers left the barest of touches, immobilizing her as she stared into his eyes. She swallowed, recognizing the tension between them. Hungry for validation that Alex wanted the same, she leaned into him moving her hands up his chest.

"This isn't allowed anymore, is it?"

Jack melted into Alex's kiss. She felt the desire and want thrashing to let loose. For the first time, Jack admitted that she would always give in to him. Thoughts of Lina, the Grand Council, and Miguel flashed through her head. None of them lasted long enough to make her pull away from him.

"What happened?" she asked catching her breath in confusion. Alex had broken off their kiss at the peak of their passion.

"I heard your thoughts and I realized that I am not being fair to you, or me." Alex's face was stern, although his fingers rubbed his lips as if in remembrance of their kiss. "I have asked a lot of you, now I ask for your trust, because a chain of events will occur that will test us all."

Jack stepped back into Alex's space. "You should already know that you have my trust."

"I do." A brief smile flitted across his face. "I confess that I initially thought that it was only you who were confused about our relationship." He paused, moving an imaginary lock from Jack's brow. "Now I know that I have been confused as well."

"You are speaking in riddles. I know that you have Lina. I know she can live forever and that makes it more attractive to be with her." Jack swallowed not wanting to admit fault, "I just..."

"Don't say it," Alex rested his forefinger on her lips, silencing her. "I know that you want more than I can give, and I know that you and Miguel have started something that you have yet to explore. I don't want to threaten that. I just can't cross that line with you until I know that it's something that we both truly want, regardless of any consequences."

Jack's smile faded. Alex's train of thought didn't ride along the same tracks as her recently departed train of thought. Miguel had been the furthest being from her mind. They may have started something, but he hadn't been around much to maintain it. They were so different. Miguel was like a slow burn and Alex more like a flash fire. "This is not about Miguel or his absence." Jack flared.

"So you are alone, too."

"It's true that he hasn't been by but—"

"Then," Alex interrupted, "this want may only be due to an unfulfilled need. I don't want you to do anything that you'll regret later."

"Alex I don't think you understand." Jack searched his eyes

"You would never have allowed this before Lina or Miguel. What has changed?"

Jack opened her mouth not finding any words that would suffice. *What had changed? Alex is still a vampire. Did that even matter anymore? Good enough to protect me; not quite good enough to be with.*

She rested her head on his chest, believing that only she knew how she truly felt. She wondered if it were real. Perhaps real for the moment would do. Her arms encircled him in a loving embrace, rather than holding on for dear life. Her smile got bigger when she felt Alex rest his lips on the top of her head and his arm wrap around her.

Jack closed her eyes and waited for the jerk that would follow, as Alex snapped his wings open and tapped times' rift.

CHAPTER SIX

The rift opened up in a long hallway, flanked with huge marble pillars leading to the entrance hall. Light blazed like hundreds of camera flashes and portals opened their magical doorways into Peace Palace.

The curved arches of the vaulted ceilings branching off in the entrance hall were softly lit by sconces on the wall. They reflected and refracted light, illuminating the length of the hallway, which appeared to never end. A large stained glass window hung over the grandiose staircase. Above, golden candelabras gave elegance to the strength and power of the hall.

Alex grabbed Jack's hand and led her down the hallway, through the sea of forming beings.

"The trial will be here?" Jack asked.

"Yes," Alex scanned the palace for Lina. He noted that Jack seemed to be more interested in absorbing the many new sights with near child-like curiosity, "The magistrates will hold council in the chambers at the end of this hallway."

Before arriving at the Great Hall, Jack tugged on Alex's suit jacket, "Where's Miguel? Isn't he supposed to be here, also?"

Alex pressed forward, taking a better grip of her hand, "I don't know where he is; he knows where he has to be."

"And Lina?"

"We'll save them seats."

"Sounds like the movies." Jack laughed.

Alex could hear her wondering if something as simple as going to the movies was in their future.

He stopped in the middle of the hallway, before the council doorway. "Remember to lock your mind."

"You heard me?" Jack's eyes widened.

Alex nodded. "And yes, we'll do many things in our time together. Some simple and others not so, let's gets through this."

"Sounds good," Jack peeked through the door.

Rows of seating, amphitheatre style, surrounded a podium and platform. Alex scanned the room, inhaling the scents for threats.

"I don't feel any malice here," he mumbled.

"Yeah, well this panther can't stop moving," Jack grumbled, "let's hurry up and find a seat."

"That panther is a ward, and we are within the Council's larger ward limiting all magic." Alex looked for a good seat. "I don't blame her for being antsy."

"How come you can still sense stuff then?" Jack queried.

Alex grinned, "I do not use magic. The ward doesn't bother me."

"That's right. I forgot the difference between animation and you."

"Thanks," Alex said with a touch of sarcasm.

"Anytime," Jack flashed a sarcastic grin.

"Let's sit here," Alex urged Jack into the seat closest to the podium. It was a pivotal point that he could protect from, with minimal people at his back.

"Saving two for Lina and Mig?"

"Right." Alex attempted to reach out for Lina mentally, but felt nothing. *Lina why do you have a block up?* Alex turned to Jack, he grin brimming with mischief. "Jack?"

"What's up?"

"Do me a favor and call Miguel?"

Jack narrowed her eyes. "Why?"

Alex could tell she was wondering what he was up to. He normally didn't care if the Archangel Michael ever showed up. "Would you just please call him?"

Jack closed her eyes and whispered, "Miguel," no sound exited her mouth, yet an unnatural whisper resounded through the hallways of Peace Palace and beyond to Miguel's ears.

Alex smiled.

"What's that for?" Jack asked looking at him.

"Lina and your angel just got here."

"What? Can you smell them?"

"I am not a blood hound. I sense them like a disturbance in the aura." Alex turned to see the mirth bubbling, like a freshly popped bottle of champagne, over Jack's face. "Be serious," he quipped with a smile. It faded as they were joined by Miguel followed by Lina.

Alex watched as Miguel sat next to Jack, and Lina crossed in front of him to sit on his left. He inhaled as she passed him.

"Good evening, my dear," Alex said pleasantly, guarding his mind while he analyzed Lina and the angel two seats over.

"Hi honey. Have the magistrate assembled yet?"

45

Alex noticed she shifted a little. He was not ready to press for an explanation. "No sweetness, you haven't missed a thing," he reached over to kiss her lips. She pulled away. "Curious."

"What is curious Amor?"

Alex watched his wife with a hawk's eye, every inflection and twitch that betrayed her nervousness. She was hiding something. "Your new scent is quite interesting, as is the taste of blood that lingers on your lips."

"Your scent is intermingled as well," Lina objected.

"Perhaps a blood exchange will help us clear things up?" Alex volunteered, lowering a fang and baring his neck. He cocked an eyebrow gauging her response.

"Soon, my love now is not a good time," Lina responded as the magistrates filed into their places.

Alex gnashed his teeth in frustration before leaving a gentle kiss atop her hand, exhaling sharply to get rid of the vanilla scent that laced her skin. "You are right, of course, my darling. Everything has a time and a place."

He sat back ignoring the discomfort of the well-worn wooden chair. He listened as the magistrates began the session, addressing minor business first. He heard Jack questioning Miguel regarding his whereabouts. Miguel was non-committal in his response. Alex forced his mind clear of all events. He needed to focus.

Something is going on. Have so many thousands of years still resulted in me being jealous? An evasive angel and an anxious wife. Paranoia is not settling in again! Alex clenched his fist. *I admit this could be a possibly manipulated situation, but something is being withheld, and I will get to the bottom of it all.*

CHAPTER SEVEN

Jack watched the court sessions commence. The defendants positioned by the podium, faced the magistrates table. Eight portentous glares dissected the presented cases. As Jack looked around the room, she observed some of the vampires that had been at the council meeting. Of the eight magistrates seated at the wooden platform table, she recognized one face.

"Alexander and Michael Archangel, approach the podium," the woman who spoke was Hecate; her skin held a pallor that was strangely luminescent. She had platinum hair and her plump, rosy lips that normally curved upwards in a smile were now thin. Her hauntingly beautiful eyes were cross, so told by her glare. She wore a white flowing robe that hinted of silver and gold. Jack would come to find out that she was the moon goddess, worshipped and followed by many witches.

"Even in anger, your beauty astounds me," Alexander swooped low in a ceremonious bow towards her. "I humbly beg your forgiveness, as I present to you the new Peace Keeper."

Jack saw Miguel roll his eyes when he took her arm before he led her to the front of the room, directly beneath the magistrate's table, which was raised by four stairs. He did not recognize Hecate as a goddess. He served his one and only, God.

An elemental seated at the left of the table spoke; her words washed across the room with a rush of wind. "Child, there are those of us that will ask you a question. You must answer all questions correctly before your Guardian can take you to the preparation room. Your answers will discern how many questions require your response."

Jack nodded, while wondering if the elemental was a ghost. She could see right through her, yet her impression was solidly placed in her mind. Her palms were sweating;

Miguel rubbed her back in reassurance. His touch was comforting and warm.

"As you stand there Child, tell me, what do you feel?" The elemental raised her hands over the expanse of the room.

Jack closed her eyes and smiled at the warmth coming from Miguel.

"I feel peace, and love, warmth and kindness."

"Archangel, un-hand the Keeper!"

The wind rushed with storm force, as the Elemental's voice boomed becoming almost solid for that angry instant. "Continue child," she said sweetly.

Jack closed her eyes again then opened them in horror at seeing the different picture behind her lids. "I feel happiness, pain, suffering with joy, anguish and love, torment and sacrifice, vindictiveness, deceit, lust, greed. Everything is all mixed up," Jack looked at the smiling elemental in confusion.

The wind was blowing in a circular motion. It faded with her smile, as the Elemental resumed her seat. Jack wondered if the Elemental had something to do with the mix of emotions that she felt.

"Peace Keeper," came the familiar voice of Ishtyn, the one face she recognized; the Lord Chancellor of the Vampire

Council, whom she met in London while masquerading as Alex's familiar.

Jack pivoted her attention to him, wondering why they passed over a man seated between him and the elemental. She wondered further, what he represented, as she was quite sure that no human sat on the bench, no matter how human they looked.

She looked at Ishtyn keenly. His thick illustrious red hair was pulled back by a band. Blue veins marked his temples, stark against his almost marble skin. Although he would never pass for human in good light, Jack was amazed at how his features enthralled her. As such, she avoided his eyes, unwilling to find herself caught in a spell, as she had when she looked into a fayerie's eyes.

"You look nervous and perhaps shaken. This world is new to you and no doubt a little overwhelming. Has anyone told you that you can refuse this position? It is, of course, a choice; a decision that only you can make. You can walk away from all of this as if it never happened. Could you make such a decision?"

Ishtyn's eyebrow was raised. A hush fell across the room, as all waited to hear the question that most dared not ask.

Jack looked down at her feet and closed her eyes. Yes, she was scared and nervous, and it was an overwhelming burden. The more she thought on it, the heavier the burden

51

became. The thought of freedom and her old life felt freeing and light. But what were the consequences of walking away? In the back of her mind, she heard Alex's voice singing to her, telling her to cross the bridge when she came to it and not before.

She dared not look around. She would bask in the refuge of the warmth of his smile, which she knew would be waiting for her. Digging into her resolve, she looked at Ishtyn defiantly. "Yes, I am scared and nervous. Public speaking is not my forte, and the burden does seem large and my shoulders small. However, I will not let fear overshadow what I feel is right. Much is unknown to me; I will cross those bridges when I come to them. I will be ready when the time comes."

Ishtyn sat down. A smile crossed his face. Jack felt Alex's smile radiating. Still juiced from the momentary spurt of adrenaline that her resolve had given her, she turned to face Hecate.

"Well-spoken, Child. Tell me about good versus evil and the light versus dark."

Jack found herself closing her eyes again as images of Miguel and Alex flashed through her head. She felt the frost of Miguel's stony scowl, while on the other side, the warmth, passion, and tenderness of Alex. More memories flashed by, this time in reversal. She shuddered when she saw Alex vamped out, consumed by anger, a smiling Miguel shielding her, as she walked along the streets of New York City, laughing and enjoying the day.

"Balance," Jack mumbled still caught up in the midst of her vision.

"Louder, Child," Hecate prompted.

"Balance. The light and the dark represent balance. Neither has anything to do with good versus evil. Good or bad can exist on either side of the light, or the dark."

Uproar came from the floor as the magical folk were divided on their reaction to her response. Jack looked around; her response was not appreciated by many. She dared not move to show that she was weak. She retreated a little bit internally, her tenacity dwindling.

"Silence!" Hecate raised her hand; her hair and robe blowing in her own personal tempest, as her power exuded from her re-gaining the order of the floor.

A clinking noise caught Jack's attention. The sound was as familiar as a fork against a wine glass, demanding a speech or kiss. She saw that it was not a fork, but the sword of the Fayerie Monarch, King Inmanethrium, that tapped a glass. She faced him respectfully.

His height, or rather, lack of it, was distracting. He waved his arms as he spoke. Jack struggled to focus by closing her eyes. One of the gifts of her new role as The Keeper was communication. When she concentrated, she could converse with all species in all tongues.

"You cannot hear? How will you be Keeper for the Fayerie when you are deaf to us?" The Fay Monarch rested his hands on his hips.

"I will learn?" Jack only caught the tail end of his question and answered him in Fayerie tongue. He was only supposed to have one question; she was hoping the last one would count. Her answer surprised even her; she was pleased when the Monarch stomped back to his seat.

She turned to the remaining two magistrates, expectantly. Although there were twelve seats, seven were filled. One of the two magistrates had long, white hair, with a youthful look. His eyes were as blue as the summer sky. When he smiled, the urge to reach out and touch him washed over Jack. She resisted the impulse to smile. The corners of her mouth twitched with reluctance.

The other magistrate was a woman who wore a collar of water that surrounded her neck. Her long, dark hair hung limply about her body. The exposed parts seemed to be covered in tiny scales rather than skin. Her eyes were shrouded in dark circles.

She smiled at Jack. Her sea green eyes were compelling, as if she were staring into an endless ocean. Jack felt as if she would go crazy staring into her eyes.

She felt Miguel's arm ushering her from the room. At the same time, she caught the gaze of King Damarius's sky blue eyes, which regarded her with more than keen interest. His look was suggestive. Jack felt a ripple along her spine as she held his gaze. Damarius was a handsome man with strong angular features that were softened by warmth that emanated from him. His eyes seemed bluer against the white of his hair, which flowed down his back. His skin held a flushed warm look that made her want to reach out and touch him again and again.

"Don't, I have to answer more questions," she whispered to Miguel, ripping her eyes away from King Damarius' hold.

"No. They are satisfied with your answers. Come."

Jack turned to see Alex step up to the podium in front of the magistrate, he did not look happy.

CHAPTER EIGHT

King Damarius of the Warlocks and Aelves stood to address Alex. His eyes had lost all feeling of summer and had become more like a wintery blizzard. He was an Aelf. With Jack gone, he relinquished his glamour. His skin took back on a pale bluish hint, and the top of his ears lost the curve and regained their signature point.

"Alexander, we meet again."

"Damarius, it is always a pleasure." Alex responded. Maintaining a smile, he bowed without taking his eyes off the king, acknowledging not Damarius's title; rather his lack of glamour as a sign of respect.

Damarius scowled at the use of his familiar name, "We are not certain that you can fulfill the role of the Keeper's Dark Angel."

"Who questions my ability?" he felt the angry darkness waiting to be called and set free.

Ishtyn rose with the briefest of hesitation. "We all do. We need to be sure that you can manage your duties in Terra, you own quite a bit of real estate. With that comes responsibility to the Vampire Council and community."

"I respectfully remind the Lord Chancellor that, that is my business and yours to question only after I fail, per our council law." Alex gritted his teeth. He never liked authority, or anyone questioning his ability.

In a rustling of garments, Hecate rose. Pointing her finger at him, her silky voice sounded soothing to Alex.

"There is not just the Vampire Council to consider now. If you intend to be a Peace Keeper's Guardian then there is the matter of timing, as to when the sub-terra estates were actually ceded to you from the sixth level daemon."

Senator Oglethorpe of the Lyanthrope, who had passed on asking any questions, stood and said in a strong Texan drawl, "Perhaps we should have a death match,"

Alex twisted his neck to crack his bones. He almost dropped a fang. He upheld his stature of dominance and control, squelching the rising fury and fighting the urge to eliminate them all. If he lost control by displaying a weakened composure, he would have to relinquish the role immediately. He'd be no good to Jack. Control was important to him. It was one of the main reasons he had lasted so many years. Dominance was typically a matter of perspective, a perspective which would only align with his own once he gained full control of any given situation.

Alex clasped his hands behind his back in a show of confidence and cleared his throat. He leveled his voice so that no trace of vampiric tone was emitted, although being charged with attempted force was far from his concern.

"There will be no death match, Senator." Alex felt Lina appear at his side. He pulled her into him. "This is my wife and she is breeding. You may have the right to pick one of us, but we'll not fight."

The magistrates sat down whispering among themselves then gasped as light filled the twelfth seat by Archangel Gabriel's presence.

Alex stared at him. Many considered him the most beautiful of all the angels. His face was feminine and smooth as a newborn baby's bottom. Alex wondered if he had the breasts of a woman, too. He was never so curious as to find out. The angel wore a light colored untailored suit that draped over him like a coat hanger, obscuring his shape.

"The candidate selected has sided with the forces of light. Although this is so, Dionysus has been known to grant a dark power that is difficult to wield. Having a sixth level daemon will grant the forces of dark too much power. We have also determined that the terra transfer happened prior to the Keeper choosing her side, thus making the vampire the appropriate choice.

"However, in the spirit of fairness, the light proposes that both enter the initiation room. Only one will be selected. The Keeper will choose, making her balance her first decision."

Having delivered his message, Gabriel left smiling at a worried Alex.

The magistrates acquiesced with the proposal. King Inmanethrium of the Fay waved his sword, sending them hurtling through a rift. They landed by a crumbling well in what appeared to be an ancient Greek garden.

"Why are you both here?" Miguel asked glancing at them before turning his attention to the well.

"Ask Gabriel," Alex answered grumpily, as he helped Lina off the ground.

Inmanethrium's sending was the equivalent of a pole toss. Alex played around with the idea of sucking his blood dry, even relishing the imagination of the cocaine equivalent high that the fayerie king would give him, as the power flushed through him.

"Where's Jack?" Alex brushed off the Grecian dirt.

"Ask Gabriel," Miguel scowled.

"What does that mean?"

"It means that Gabriel took off with her."

"Are you not her Warrior of Light? What means did you take to protect her from Gabriel's absconding?" Alex paced around him.

So many circumstances beyond his control were taking place. He expected everyone on the same team to share the same goals. How could Miguel simply let Gabriel run off with Jack? "Was there nothing within your ability that you sought to do?"

Alex watched the stony face of the angel cloud with rage.

"Gabriel is a Warrior of Light. He would not hurt Jack."

"Gabriel is a messenger. He will only fulfill his duties. You are assigned to protect Jack." Fury rippled through Alex like an August heat wave.

"I have faith—"

Alex cut Miguel off by placing his hand around the angel's throat producing yelling and screaming from Lina. "Did you at least ask where he took her?" Alex pressed ignoring Lina's incessant screams.

"I did," Miguel grabbed Alex's arm and applied pressure to his elbow with his other hand.

Alex countered his maneuver and dodged as Miguel drew his sword from the invisible sheath on his back. When not in use the sword appeared as a simple tattoo on the angel's back. When he drew it became an extension of flaming angelic fury. "And he said?"

"Nothing," came Miguel's gruff reply drawing his strength to swing his blade again.

"I don't know how you protect your women, but letting them get taken by a stranger to somewhere beyond your ability to follow, and outside of your knowledge is not my idea of protection."

Miguel growled, flared his wings and aimed his sword. "Gabriel is no stranger; I have known him for millennia."

Alex could hear Lina yelling in the background. Her incessant screams had no impact. In fact, they only seemed to help ignite the fire. Alex's fury with Miguel partially encompassed the lack of knowledge regarding their involvement with each other, and what he presumed to be a lack of judgment on Miguel's part regarding his care for Jack.

"Gabriel is not on our team. However, we each are on Jack's team and we're supposed to have one goal, protect her. Do you really believe that he has her best interests at heart? As a matter of fact, do you want what's best for her?

On a personal note, I thought you and she were an item. What is going on with you?" Alex's extended his fangs and unsnapped his wings. He felt each talon sliding along his fingers until his hands became predatory claws.

"C'mon guys," Lina screamed. "This is not what we should be doing right now. Alex, please don't hurt Miguel. I'm sure there's an explanation."

Alex growled ignoring his wife. He sprung upwards, and launched at Miguel.

CHAPTER NINE

"Well can you at least give me a map?" Jack screamed. Her clenched fists hit her legs, as she watched the back of Gabriel's head disappear consumed by the bushes. Turning, she narrowed her eyes to analyze her surroundings. Tall austere hedges lined every direction. She realized she had been left in the center of a maze, with a small clearing at best, with a worn marble bench that probably showed up in every Dracula movie ever produced.

Jack felt the panther begin pacing across her shoulder blades, a sure sign of its uneasiness. "I know and I hear you;

I just don't know what to do about it." Jack gave one last look around and set forward. "I don't know if this is the right direction, but it's a direction. I'm not going to get anywhere standing still." The wolf uncurled itself from her thigh, positioning itself on her hip.

She moved forward with caution, down one of the aisles lined with tall foreboding hedges. She trailed her hands over the leaves as she walked. Her pace was purposeful. "Something is watching us guys."

I don't know why I keep speaking to you like you are going to speak back to me. Her laugh lightened her spirits a little; her senses stayed on edge.

A low growl rumbled through the hedges. The branches trembled. Jack spun around, only to find leaves falling through the air.

Her eyes focused on the path of a single leaf gliding through the air in a slow descent. Flitting from side to side as it navigated its way to the ground. Each shift left Jack feeling as if doom were upon her. "Aegis," Jack whispered. "Aegis, get us out of here."

She backed up, waiting for Aegis' mist to surround her. Instead, she felt an irritation on her left shoulder blade. Her wolf tattoo had made its way up to her shoulder and threw its nose upwards in a long silent howl. Its ward was released. "I guess we're limited here. It's okay Aegis, I got this one."

Jack backed up with great haste, turned and went into a full speed run. She looked over her shoulder to see more leaves falling, and she heard the growl grow louder.

The earth trembled beneath her feet. Looking over her shoulder once again, she saw from her peripheral view, a dark being bursting through the hedges into the pathway she was running down.

"Oh shit! A bull cat thing. What on earth is that?"

She saw red eyes and large horns protruding out of the front of its forehead. Big cat feet allowed the animal to move with ease, as it covered the ground between them.

"Shit, shit, shit," Jack increased her speed, barely looking where she was going. Her right foot caught on an iron ring jutting out from of the ground sending her flying head over heels.

Her hands hit the ground, throwing her into a forward roll. Her back finally landed against an ill-placed marble bench. A silver platter landed on her lap. She looked up in the direction the platter came from, seeing two other objects hurtling towards her; she calculated the speed of their descent, catching one object in her right hand and the other in her left.

"Ow!" she exclaimed letting go of the object in her right hand, finding it too hot to hold.

Jack watched as a reddish, egg-shaped object rolled down her, onto the ground. Inertia rolled the egg alongside her right splayed leg, towards a little red figure she hadn't seen before.

Jack's eyes widened in horror at seeing the bull-like creature lower its horns, aiming towards the figure that stood in the middle of the aisle. An iron shackle hung loosely over the little red figure's head.

Jack assumed she tripped over the chain draping from the shackle that lay twisted at her foot. "Ugh! Now the figure was in danger. "No!" she screamed and put her hand up to warn the red figure that stood staring at her with its head cocked to the side.

It turned to face the charging beast that skidded to a halt in front of the fearless figure. The beast snorted and pranced.

Jack called out to the little being asking it to run or be careful. She swore she heard a growl from the red figure, but wasn't sure. Confusion set in when the large bull-like creature gave a high pitched yelp and took off through the hedges leaving Jack and the little red figure alone in the aisle of the maze. She eyed the figure. The feeling of panic and the need to flea vanished for the moment. She noticed that, although small, it was feminine and almost human, if it were not for the red skin. Long, rabbit looking ears pointed upwards through its unruly, straight hair. The skin covering the abdomen was lighter in color, almost pink, like a dog's underbelly, although the hands and feet were covered in tiny scales. Jack realized that the whole body was covered in scales, though the hands had feet had larger more recognizable scales.

"Hi," Jack said, taking a chance that it was friendly, "so sorry for tripping over you. Why are you chained up?"

The little being smiled.

She noticed her eyes were completely yellow, and her teeth were sharp and fanged like no animal she had ever seen. Each tooth was pointed with spaces between them. She watched the little being as she strained against her chains to pick up the red egg. The weight of the other object made an impression, Jack stared at it. She realized she was holding a blue egg that matched the red one the little being had. A liquid was inside. She held it up. Iridescence covered the egg; but Jack could make out a figure inside.

She stared at the little being on her tether cradling the red egg then offered it the palm sized iridescent blue egg. Being only about three feet tall, she struggled with nestling the eggs in the crook of her arms.

"Thanks."

Jack smiled. "You speak. What are you?"

"Dhjinn,"

"Dragon?" Jack queried thinking that the little dhjinn probably had not used its voice in a long time. It sounded coarse and rough.

The dhjinn grinned, shrugging her shoulders. A little flame and smoke flickered between her teeth. She covered her mouth partially with one hand; cradling the egg with the other.

Jack got back to her feet. "Do you know the way out?"

The dhjinn nodded, but cast a forlorn glance at her restraints.

Jack removed the large iron shackle from the dhjinn's head. "I'm not sure why you couldn't get out of this yourself, you know." The shackle lifted without even touching a hair. "It's not like it even touched you. I mean it's like trying to run thread through a basketball hoop."

The dhjinn smiled.

Jack stared in amazement as the dhjinn burst into flames. Seconds after the shock dissipated, she realized that the little being had disappeared. She was now left alone in the maze staring at settling smoke where it once stood.

"Great!" she brushed the silt off her pants and got to her feet. "Well, I guess sitting here isn't going to help."

She pulled out her cell phone and tapped on the screen. Eight hours had elapsed since she encountered the being and started walking. Her footsteps had begun to drag an eternity ago. Her muscles ached and micro sleep was taking over in the unchanging landscape of tall austere hedges. For eight hours she had not been able to make a turn. Not a left or a right had cropped up. She had even tried barging through the bushes like the bull-like creature had, but it just wasn't feasible. The bushes just seemed to squeeze her out.

As her eyes faltered, she imagined that she was walking through the streets in Brooklyn, flanked by the brownstones of New York. She shook her head in disbelief. "Did those buildings just move?" Jack put her hand to her head. "Whoa, my head hurts."

Scanning the street, Jack spied a park-bench by a bus stop. She sighed in relief and made a bee-line for it. Checking both directions, she didn't see anyone, or anything. She sat on the bench. The moment she touched the chair the remaining energy drained out from her.

"Alex, I think you're going to have to come get me now." A little air formed her words making the request barely audible, before she slipped into an unconscious state.

She wasn't aware that the dhjinn appeared baring its teeth. Its red ears flattened to the side of its head. Moving towards the park-bench with bared fangs, smoke exited its mouth and nose.

CHAPTER TEN

"We have bigger worries. Fighting amongst ourselves will not resolve anything," Lina stood with one palm on Miguel's chest and the other on Alex's.

Alex backed away. He didn't take his eye off Miguel, who reluctantly moved out of his offensive pose.

"So, now that you guys are not going to fight, do we just sit here and wait?" Lina grumbled.

"There's nothing we can do besides wait until we are called." Alex regarded his wife with growing suspicion. His eyes glanced between her and the archangel. "Since I have both of you here as a captive audience, I must ask a question. Why is it that the two of you always seem to be wearing an infusion of the other's scent?

Alex noticed the furtive glance Miguel cast to Lina. He also noticed the instant smile that graced his wife's face, as she sauntered towards him crooning.

"Aww baby, are you jealous?"

Alex didn't let his guard down. "Not typically. You must be spending a lot of time together for your scent to blend together so." Alex went on as she pressed herself against him. He stared at Miguel; he knew the angel couldn't lie.

"Honey, that's so flattering," Lina persevered. "There's nothing going on between Miguelito and I, he's just helping me out with a few things."

Alex noted a change in Miguel's face to a stony unreadable mask. "Very well, I won't press the issue, as of yet." Alex looked down at her, wondering what they were hiding.

The faintest whisper caught his attention. "Jack!" Alex pushed Lina firmly aside.

"Miguel, take Lina and head towards the GMA. I'll meet you there with Jack." Alex snapped his wings and tapped a rift upon receipt of a confirmation nod from Miguel.

The call seemed to come from the land of Dark Fay. As he traveled through time's rift, Alex couldn't help but muse upon the fact that he had received no objections from the grumpy angel. Something had changed the relationship between him and Lina.

Closing his wings against the impact of bursting through the rift, he shielded himself against a burst of flame as he exited. A shot of adrenaline blasted through him. Hunger hit him like a blast from an energy drink.

Dark fay were crawling all over. A fire-breathing dragon stood guarding Jack. Alex mustered his control and dropped his fangs. He channeled his anger, drawing upon both the darkness and the light within him for balance and plunged into the fray. He snapped his wings open and bellowed in anger. The glamour dropped, once again becoming nothing more than an aisle in the maze between the hedges.

Sensing fear, he spun around to locate the fayerie that put the glamour in place. A swipe of his hand took the unsuspecting fayerie's head and sent it rolling. Pungent blood splattered over him. His eyes turned red and he knew his control was threatened. The fay ran screaming, knowing what would happen to them in the vicinity of such a powerful vampire overcome by blood lust. Their fun was over.

Alex turned to look at the dragon. It stood guarding Jack. Smoke emanated from its nostrils. "You have guarded her well, dhjinn. I have to take her to the GMA, where she will be safe."

Tremors ran through Alex, and he fought against the desire to tear the place apart. He hated the effect the fay had on him. He watched the dragon dissipate into a smoky haze. Exhausted, the little dhjinn flopped on top of Jack. Alex strode over and scooped them up; the dhjinn nestled on top of her.

"Hold on," he said, as he tapped the rift to the GMA. He wondered if he was urging himself, or them.

Landing in the gardens of Peace Palace, Alex found Miguel and Lina waiting for him. With undue haste, he dropped them into Miguel's arms and tapped the rift back to the Macedo tower.

A low growl reminded him he was home.

"Down boy," he mumbled heading straight to the refrigerator. He knocked a ham hock onto the floor that Jesus, the hell-hound, dived into. Alex stumbled to his bathroom having grabbed a bag of blood from the fridge. He stuck it in his mouth piercing the bag with his fangs. He closed his eyes in relief, feeling for the light switch while listening to the sounds of ripping flesh coming from the kitchen.

Staring in the mirror, he saw the side of his blackened face regenerating. "Burned by that damned dhjinn", he mumbled with the bag of blood still in his mouth. Alex shook his head. "Dammit Jack! Why didn't you call me sooner?" He peered at the red eyes staring back at him. Grabbing a wash cloth and running it under water, Alex attempted to remove the fay blood coating his face. Filling the wash basin with water he submerged his head feeling the sweet relief of the purifying water. A new scent permeated the water. He withdrew his head with fangs bared, the bag of blood still hanging from his mouth.

"I don't know whether the dhjinn was damned or not. I do think that the Keeper was quite fortunate to befriend the young dhjinn, and that the youngster had the power to transform into a dragon at such an early age."

Alex twisted in the direction of the voice. Yanking the bag from his mouth, he called, "Athena?"

"Have you forgotten so quickly, Alexander?"

Her voice dripped like honey, although Alex was not so foolish to believe that she was coming on to him. "Not at all my lady."

"You almost lost the Keeper today."

Alex lowered his eyes in agreement. Athena was truly beautiful, as well as wise. He did not want to be blinded, or left in any worse condition than he was.

"You hesitated in the garden."

"Something is amiss between that angel and the prince." Alex used Lina's title to avoid any emotional considerations.

"Perhaps, but of no consequence if the Keeper cannot be guarded," Athena reminded him.

"The fates are out of control. Destinies are unclear and muddled." Alex started.

"Have a care Alexander," Athena cautioned. "Sometimes too much control is just as devastating as too little."

Gunshots caught their attention. "The penthouse," Alex looked at Athena. "Please, I am still weak. I could use your help."

Alex grabbed Athena's hand, as she reached out to him. They appeared in the penthouse to find the hot rain of bullets showering down upon them. Alex roared as the slugs bit into him. Both strategists, Athena and Alex split up disarming the thug's weaponry in no time.

"Max?" A sense of urgency welled up in Alex's chest. "I can feel you, but I cannot find you."

The elevator bell dinged and an ear splitting scream gave Max's location.

"Hurry Alex, his spirit is traveling," Athena called to him.

With preternatural speed, Alex made it to Max's side, moving a screaming Sam back into Miguel's arms. He realized that Jack, Sam, and Miguel were the reason the elevator doors had opened.

Alex raised Max's head, examining the damage to his son's mortal body. Blood tears fell freely down his checks, splashing onto Max's face. The transfer of energy gave Max enough will to take a deep breath. The blood of a vampire could heal a human from all, but mortal injuries.

"Father," Max's whisper came.

"My son."

"I'm not ready to go, Father," Max smiled at him. "I hear her voice running through me. I don't want to leave either of you yet."

Alex looked over his shoulder, passed Athena to see Jack and Miguel restraining Sam, the love of his son's natural life.

"Things may change, son."

"Everything changes, Dad."

Amidst the screams from Sam begging him to save Max, and pleading with him not to change him, Alex let out the most painful roar, baring his fangs before sinking them into Max's neck.

Alex watched his body went into convulsions. He split open his wrist with a fang and allowed the blood to spill into his mouth. "Wake my son." His voice was filled with a heavy sadness. "Wake truly as my son."

Alex could hear Sam's screams give way to sobs. A feeble grip on his hand diverted his attention back to Max, and he pressed his open wound to Max's mouth. "Drink."

A few minutes passed and Alex wrenched his wrist away from Max. "That's enough." The force sent Max sliding backwards into the window. Alex sank into the couch feeling weak.

"Max?"

Alex turned to see Sam trying to get out of Miguel's grip. He could see that Max was responding to her call.

"Sam, not yet," Alex held up his hand in warning; Sam didn't appear to be listening.

A bright light pierced the room sending Max hurtling backwards into the shadows. Miguel drew his sword and stood in all his angelic glory, ready to protect Sam and Jack.

Alex got up. "Okay Miguel, turn the light down a notch. I'm up. I'm going to take Max to Augy. Davern will be here to clean up."

"You are going to move a fledgling during the daylight hours?" Athena mused. "What a bold move."

"We don't have time to waste in waiting," Alex looked at her.

"Remember my words Alexander." Athena cautioned before changing into her familiar owl shape, and flying off through one of the broken windows.

"What was that all about?" Jack queried.

"A long story for another time," Alex reached into his pocket, extracted his cell phone and dialed. Seeming satisfied with the response, he ended the call.

"Davern?" Miguel asked.

"Yes." Alex looked at Jack longingly. "Stay safe for me, please."

"Who is Davern? "He's a cleaner. You'll meet him soon enough," Alex smiled.

Jack walked confidently over to Alex. "You too," she looked up into his eyes, "You stay safe also."

Alex felt Jack's arms encircle his torso. He looked at Miguel begging for strength. "Jack. I'm weakened. I have to go." Alex could feel the darkness rising in the pit of his stomach. Mustering all of his control, he squelched the sound of her heartbeat and lowered his lips to hers. "Just call me if you need me. You know I'll come."

Alex released his hold on Jack when he sensed an increase in Miguel's presence.

The elevator doors opened, allowing Blondie to rush through with his gun targeted everywhere.

Alex moved to his side picking the man up by the jaw while disarming him. "Where in hell have you been?"

"Sir, I was knocked out. Five floors down, we were breached and I stumbled upon them. The last thing I remember is someone saying, *make sure you don't forget to tell*

Macedo. And a note was stuffed in my mouth. I think they gave me something. I must have passed out, sir."

Alex scented the fear running through Blondie, as well as the remaining odor of Benzophene. He lowered him to the floor. "Call Davern with the particulars."

"Sir, yes sir." Blondie stood at attention acknowledging his task, as he whipped out his cell phone, immediately taking a count of the bodies providing an assessment of the situation.

Alex flipped open his cell phone, too. "Augy, get me a surgeon, and some food. I'm coming with a baby vamp."

The elevator bell indicated the arrival of the cleaning crew.

"Perfect timing, Davern you will notate the birth of my son," Alex bellowed, as he turned to Miguel, "You will keep them safe until my return."

Davern nodded. "I haven't been here in a while Macedo, what do we have?"

"Blondie should have given you the particulars… But at a high level; clean up Davern. Human remains, one window, the following are live and also need attention. The police will be here shortly. One witch, one keeper, and one angel."

"Eww, an angel. I haven't had one of those in years." Davern muttered.

Max's body started twitching and shuddering, as he gasped for air, his hands were around his throat. His body struggled to function, requiring more blood to sustain the vampiric organisms coursing throughout him.

"Davern, do you note his birth?" Alex yelled. He grabbed Max's hands pinning them, as he cupped his chin with the other hand to bare his fangs.

CHAPTER ELEVEN

"I do, one Maxwell Macedo born New York Eastern Region. Sire – Alexander."

Alex watched Davern, as he notated the event in his monotonous voice and began giving instructions: who needed to go where and do what. Sensing time was of the essence; Alex shifted Max out of the tower, shielding him from the light with his wings in the rift, as they moved through the rift tunnel to Russia. Because he was an older vamp mixed with daemonic blood, the light proved to be an irritation. They moved fast. The UVB rays didn't have a chance to do any damage; to any other vampire, especially those newly formed in the afterlife, it would be a slow painful death, as the UVB rays burned the flesh off the barely regenerated body.

The rift broke through in the center of the Russian palatial conference room. Alex had once addressed the inhabitants of the palace when he assumed control of the Russian territory, killing the enemy of the Vampire Council, Lars, a self-proclaimed victor over Russian territory. He was incensed by Xylar's interference into Were and Vampire business.

Xylar had been the right-hand man for the devil himself after Lina had gone missing. Lina was Catalina De Diablo the daughter of the devil, crowed Prince of Hell, and betrothed to Alex until she went missing. Much mystery still existed about the historic chain of events and how they were all linked, but Xylar and Lina were each at one end, or the other.

Xylar was also the daemon who originally marked Jack as a daemon bride, a title she did not relish having. Alex stole her or, rather, set her free when he escaped from hell on one occasion, not for his own purposes; rather just to free an innocent victim. They had become more than good friends since then. At the end of the day, Xylar died at Alex's hands in a battle over Lina, leaving him as the titled Underlord for both the sixth and fifth levels of hell.

Augy was waiting for Alex holding a skittish chestnut mare. Her ears laid flat in fear, or surprise. Her eyes wild, as the rift broke open with Alex and Max. Sunlight streamed into the room through the filtered digital windows. Max darted out of Alex's grasp to the back of the room, hiding in the shadows as preternatural instinct for survival took over. His body craved the darkness where his mind told him it would be safe.

Alex took a look towards the double doors to the conference hall, they were open. Channeling a blast of air, he sent them flying shut. He walked towards Augy with his arms opened, casting a quick glance at Max checking on his disposition. He mentally scanned the area.

"Augy, it is so good to see you," Alex gave him a full embrace, releasing him as he felt the tug from the Mare on Augy's arm.

"Good to see you too, boss," Augy grinned toothily. His incisors were naturally a little longer than usual, even when fully retracted. "Even if under the circumstances. I'm sorry to hear about the boy, boss. Maybe it was always in his future."

"She's pretty. Is she for Max?" Alex asked eyeing up the Mare, not quite ready to acknowledge the change in Max.

Could the events be considered the loss of a human son, or the gain of a vampiric one? Either way, Alex was still on edge, so much could go wrong with a fledgling vampire. Max had it so much worse. His life was one integrated with human companionship. He would have to fight the urge for thirst for the next hundred years, until he learned control. Would he even be able to see Sam again before she died of old age? Alex sighed. *So much to think about, given the decision.*

"Yeah, all we could do on such short notice. Unless you want some of the people brought in here?" Augy quirked an eyebrow.

"No, he was low on blood before the transfer, and he took a lot of blood from me. Old blood mixed with Lina's. Mind you it has been a moment since we did a full exchange."

"Trouble in paradise, boss?"

Alex glanced at Augy, realizing he had opened himself up for the question and the second time he had heard the reference to paradise. He opted to ignore it. "I don't want to give him human blood yet. Not until he has learned some control over his abilities." Alex mused. "Let's take her over to him. A shame though, she has some nice lines." Alex allowed his mind to drift to the mare, but quickly turned back to the business of preparing Max for the new world that he was going to become a part of.

Alex and Augy started towards the corner where Max was crouched in the corner. The mare was getting skittish, sensing death with every step. She pulled back on the tether, backing, making shrill whinnying noises and tossing her head frantically to free herself. She tried to rear upwards; she was no match for Augy's vampiric strength. The mare tossed her head, pawing the marble floors.

Alex focused on Max, as he tensed his body, ready to catch the young vamp should he try to get around them. *The making of a vampire is not as romantic as the movies depict.* Alex caught Augy nodding in agreement as they moved forward uniformly.

****

Max turned to stare at them, his eyes wide and his face showing fear. His incisors bared and he pulled his lips back hissing; all rational thought eradicated as the primordial instinct of survival dominated his new afterlife.

Max changed his defensive crouch to an offensive one. He could barely see, and tried to adjust to his new preternatural eyesight. He made out three figures walking towards him. There was so much noise; he couldn't distinguish any intelligible words. So many new sounds were open to him with the heightened level of hearing. He couldn't block the sounds out; he felt like he was going crazy.

As the figures came closer, a whooshing sound became louder. Max closed his eyes and covered his ears, crouching defensively again. The sound became more of a whoosh thump. His eyes flew open, as he inhaled several times quickly. The scent of sweat and fear incensed him. His body went on cruise control; his instincts took over.

Alex and Augy stopped a couple of meters in front of him. He saw Alex turned a mare's head sideways baring her neck. Max stood up on shaky legs. He moved cautiously towards the animal, avoiding staring at Alex and Augy, though he cast furtive glances at them. He was drawn by the fear coursing through the creature. As he got closer, Augy increased his grip, which sent a bolt of fear shooting through her. She struggled. The shockwave of fear overcame Max, his senses feeding off of the emotion, exciting him. Not able to withstand the un-curtailed desire, he lunged, sinking his new fangs into the mare's neck. The blood squirted into his mouth, warm and thick.

"Max, feel the pulse of the blood. Draw it slowly. It will come. Take your time." Alex reached over to him holding the back of his neck with one hand, as he felt for the horse's pulse with the other. "Son, listen to me, feel for the rhythm of the blood. Draw it slowly, match the rhythm. You must stop before the last beat of the heart. This is important, most of all. You must stop before the heart beat its last beat."

Though he was feeling a little heady, Alex's words were sinking in, as his rationale kicked back in with the flow of blood. He felt the blood pumping into him, the feel of the whooshing and thumping flow of the heartbeat. It was like a melody playing. The animal's memories flashed through him, as he drew its life's forces. She had been carefree as a filly, taken from her mother too early and placed in an unfamiliar barn. Her memories flashed by like an old reel movie. Finally, it dawned on him that he was drawing blood from a horse and he felt repulsed. Max threw himself backwards, hitting the wall not understanding his own strength.

"It's okay. You're probably feeling a little sick." Alex knelt in front of him. The pallor had returned to Max's face.

Max pointed at the weakened beast. "That's a horse. I drank the blood," he blubbered, spitting fur out of his mouth.

Augy laughed. "Yes you did my little mosquito."

Max's stomach churned. He began convulsing with dry heaves.

Alex sat down next to him patting him on the back. "This too is normal. You must make peace with yourself, otherwise this will happen every day and it will hurt like a son-of-a-bitch. You are a vampire now. This is what you must do to survive. It will take about six months before you have full control over yourself and maybe one hundred years before you have full control over the thirst. Just know that that's six months before you can see Sam alone if you don't get it together. The sooner you come to terms with this change, the easier it will be. You don't want to wait one hundred years before you can see her do you?"

At the mention of Sam's name, Max drew in a sharp breath.

"Breathe out," Alex told him. "Breathing is not really necessary, but recommended if you live around humans. It makes them feel comfortable and makes talking easier. Even though it is not required, don't hold your breath inside, it gets stale. Bad breath kills."

Max exhaled. His eyes opened wide at Alex's last statement. He cast an inquiring glance up at Augy, who laughed in return.

"A joke," Alex chuckled, crossing his legs wincing as the pain from one the bullets pressed on a nerve. "Take some more, you need it."

Max got up, still unsure of what it took to make his body work. His new strength made him feel as if he were a baby all over again, learning how to walk, talk, see, think, hear, and eat.

"Help him out." Alex waved his hand at Augy who stopped smiling and became serious.

Max took a glance towards Alex. He appeared to be extracting a bullet from the back of his hand with an extended fang. The sound of the mare's grunting and fresh scent of blood brought Max's focus back. He saw Augy give the mare's puncture wounds a squeeze. Max felt his incisors move. He ran his tongue over his teeth, feeling their sharpness. His eyes fluttered. Lust overwhelmed him. Driven, he moved towards the mare, only to find Augy's hand on his forehead.

"Max, if you don't learn to control it now, it will always control you." Augy cautioned. Holding his head with the flat of his palm, he stared into Max's feral eyes.

The fire that had begun to flare quelled and his internal struggle began.

"Your body is a shell, but it has needs. You are so strong up here." Augy jabbed his index finger into his head repeatedly. "When you want to do something fast, do it slow so you can control it. Savor the pain that comes with waiting. Your receptors will become numb after a while. The sooner you learn this, the sooner you can resume much of a normal life."

A dull recognition floated through Max's brain. He remembered Sam's giggle now fading into a whisper like a forgotten memory. The smell of blood tingled in his nostrils replacing his love for Sam with new memories of lust – for blood. He rolled his eyes toward the mare then rolled his shoulders back. "I'm good. I'm full," he panted a few shallow breaths and glanced surreptitiously at Alex who had risen, and was, to his surprise, staring at him with a slow smile cracking an otherwise stony stare.

"Why are you staring at me like that?" Max whispered with a lisp. His incisors were in the way. He was conscious of his inability to retract them.

"Channel your breath. You will find more than a whisper. Oh, and push them with your finger, you will feel the sensation of them sliding back. Learn that feeling and you will control them, too," Alex answered.

Max complied. Satisfied with the results, he vowed to remember the feeling.

Alex beckoned for him and Augy to follow him then added, "Leave the horse Augy, have someone come for it."

"Why were you staring?" Max yelled, not yet able to gauge the amount of air required to talk normally. "Sorry." He whispered raising his eyebrows apologetically as Alex paused mid-stride to look at him. Max saw amusement bubbling in his preternatural eyes.

"It was a good decision, son." Alex answered simply before turning to Augy. "Aug, where is that surgeon. These pellets are making me irritable," he reached into his pocket and extracted the note he had taken from Blondie. "I want to talk shop. We have a leak and I want the hole plugged." Pushing the note back into his pocket, he followed Augy.

CHAPTER TWELVE

The rain of bullets came showering down on the marine as he waded his way through the swampy marsh grass in North Korea. A bomb exploded nearby, sending marshy dirt splattering over him. The marine flattened himself to the earth pausing to make sure he had not been hit. Rising to a crouch he surveyed the area through the dust and smoke filled jungle.

Another loud explosion mirrored Sam's blood curling scream, it was a perfect fit for any horror movie.

Blondie paused the movie and Sam, Lina, Jack, and Miguel turned around on the couch with their hands thrown up in feigned frustration.

"Hey, what's going on?" Lina asked, "Why did you stop the movie?"

"Mrs. Macedo there is a detective here," Blondie mumbled.

Lina saw a plain clothed policeman push Blondie aside and walked down the stairway. He was followed by his partner.

She eased up off the couch, her belly becoming more of a nuisance with each month. "I didn't even hear the elevator ding," her voice started off lightly until she saw it was Detective Edward Trattoria. She'd met him at the police station as a suspect in the murder of her human lover, Carlos Fiores, just before she married Alex and was introduced to Jack and Sam.

Edward had his nose in his notebook as he walked towards her. "Good afternoon Mrs. Macedo, I'm Edward Trattoria and I'm looking for Max Macedo, are you his wife?" Ed looked at her, squinting his eyes.

"Oh no," Lina smiled, "I'm his step-mother. Can I help you?"

Ed returned a brief smile. "We got a complaint of gunshots. We have a witness who said someone died?"

"Oh dear, that's terrible. When and where did this happen?" Lina asked furrowing her brows while she placed one hand on her mouth and the other on her belly protectively. "I must talk to my husband. I told him this neighborhood was going downhill."

Ed cocked his head as if they were speaking at cross purposes. "Uh, ma'am. Our witness says that the murder happened here."

Lina laughed, fanning her face with a hand, and rubbing her belly with the other. "I thought for a moment you were serious about the murder," Lina told him, still chuckling.

"I am. Do you mind if we look around?" Ed stared at her snapping on his gum. He gave her a serious look from under his eyebrows.

"Your friend has been looking around the room as we've been speaking. There has been no murder here. It's just been us having a movie night."

"If you don't mind me looking around," Ed's voice trailed, as he noticed Jack and Sam on the couch.

"Of course, you can look around Detective. Let me see your warrant so I know what you are looking for and you can do your thing. You won't mind if we continue our movie?" Lina smiled extending her hand.

"We don't have a warrant right now, but I can get one." He looked at Lina then waved to Jack and Sam, who waved back. "How rude of me, good afternoon ladies."

"Hi Ed," Jack and Sam said in unison.

"Excuse me Detective?" Lina smiled.

Ed swung his attention back to her.

"I just have a quick question that might save us all some trouble."

Ed clasped his hands in front of him.

Lina watched him glance at Jack and Sam. She was sure he was wondering who the mysterious friend was and why he hadn't been introduced to Miguel.

"Have you, by chance, been talking to Ms. Robinson from across the way in the neighboring tower? You know sometimes she just sees things through that telescope of hers that aren't quite right." Lina smiled again tapping her head with her index finger and throwing her voice a little louder, so that both detectives paid attention. She had taken the liberty of slipping into their minds to retrieve the name of their informant.

"I'm not at liberty to discuss where we got our tip," Ed said, not wanting to acknowledge an apparent failure.

"Oh, no problem. I understand police business." Lina whispered. "I watch the crime scene shows all the time. I was just curious, because we just finished watching

Underworld Evolution and there is a lot of gunfire and death. There is this one guy with wings that gets killed like how many times," Lina was giving herself a headache trying to babble.

"Ma'am, thank you for your time," Ed was being pulled discretely by his partner, Louie. "If we need anything else, we'll be sure to come back with a warrant." Ed shot Lina his best police detective smile.

"As you wish, Detective," Lina was quite thankful that she didn't have to keep up the conversation any longer.

She watched as he walked towards the stairs in the direction of the elevator then raised her eyebrows and forced a smile when he stopped and turned towards her.

"Would you mind if I had a quick word with Ms. Brunson?" Ed raised his eyebrow in question as his eyes flitted from Lina to Jack.

She waved her hand towards Jack. "I cannot speak for her; perhaps you should ask her yourself?"

Lina watched Jack get up from the couch without waiting for Ed's request. She stuck her hands in the back pockets of her jeans. She smiled, knowing that Jack's hands always sweat when she told a lie, so she didn't want to touch him.

"Hey Eddie, how are you?"

Lina mused at the tone in Jack's voice, her smile was genuine.

"Jack, where have you been? What are you doing here?" Ed hissed at her trying to keep his voice down.

"What are you talking about? I've been out of town for a bit and I'm watching the movies with some friends. Is that a crime?"

"Jack, there is a warrant for your arrest. You left your car on the wrong side of the street. The sweeper came, you got several tickets. You never paid them. Your car has been impounded. You haven't claimed it. I stopped by, but there was no answer. Have you been home yet? Did you pay your rent? You have an eviction notice waiting for you. What is going on with you? This is so not like you," Lina could hear Ed whispering with such urgency that he was almost spitting out his words.

"Oh shit! I thought I had given the landlord due notice," Jack exclaimed, "I hadn't realized about the car though. I haven't really had a need for it lately." Jack added.

"I'm going to bring you in and we'll figure out everything, okay?" Ed shook his head in disbelief taking out his cuffs.

"Dude, you're gonna use cuffs?" Louie interjected. "After all, its jus parking tickets an' ya know perhaps a misunnerstanding."

"Eddie, I'll go with you. Cuffs aren't necessary; if you're worried go ahead. I won't hold it against you." Jack lost her smile.

Ed shook his head and motioned for her to follow Louie.

"Jack, we are coming with you," Lina looked at Miguel and Sam who nodded in agreement. Lina then turned to Blondie. "B, get a car please."

A change in air alerted her to a new presence. "Miguel, why don't you get everyone in the car and I'll meet you in the garage. I have to pee." She caressed her belly for good measure.

Satisfied that everyone had left, Lina put her hands on her hips. "Hello Daddy dearest," she snarled.

"Don't you daddy dearest me," Lucifer materialized in front of her.

"What do you want?" she snapped.

"I'm here to give you a warning."

"A warning?" Lina regarded her father's furrowed brows knitted in anger. In human form, the telltale tick of a blood vessel pulsated on his forehead. She decided not to aggravate him further. "What can I do for you, Daddy?"

"You were either supposed to get the position of the Keeper, or you were supposed to end up as the Keeper's guardian." Lucifer bared his teeth. "You are letting your..." his voice trailed while he made circular antics with his hand to show he was looking for a choice word. Settling, he continued, "You are letting your condition impact the plans."

"Father, we agreed that should an opportunity present itself, I would make such moves. However, my dear husband is quite a strategist and is always one step ahead of the game." Lina smiled.

"Are you telling me that as the rightful Prince of the Underworld you are unable to match, or best your husband? Lucifer queried.

Lina scowled, her accent was thick from frustration, "I'm reminding you that your blood courses through Alejandro as it does mine. We have positioned him to make moves in our best interest.

Lucifer flipped his hand in disgust. "Bah!"

Lina breathed a sigh of relief as her father disappeared. The last of his voice filtered to her to apply caution.

The elevator dinged, "I'm coming," she yelled as she moved towards the staircase.

CHAPTER THIRTEEN

The police station hummed like an ant hill. Police officers milled about securing the chain of custody for found evidence. Those who had been Mirandized were broadcasting their innocence and all unjust actions levied against them to all who would listen. A few unified with those with similar crimes hoping for strength in numbers.

Jack scanned the faces, still waiting to be booked. She wondered how many of the quiet ones were innocent of crimes and simply a victim of acquaintance, or bad timing.

She watched the police swell in numbers to subdue a belligerent who was banging his head against an officer's desk.

"Jack."

Ed Trattoria's voice pierced her focus.

"What's up Ed?"

"I have to take you back to holding until the bench warrant can be lifted."

"Why, is there something wrong with the check they gave you?"

"No, but it has to clear processing. Its protocol I'm sure you understand."

"Whatever." Jack rolled her eyes. Ed clearly was not making anything easier for her. She caught Lina's eye. "You okay?" she mouthed.

She shook her head, no.

Jack trained her thoughts in on Lina, her pallor was becoming shallow. "Miguel?"

Miguel turned.

"You have to get Lina out of here. Something's not right with her."

"She is struggling with the amount of fresh blood in circulation," Miguel divulged.

"Ask Sam to get her some of that new stuff she's been trying to practice on Alex. Maybe it'll help."

"What about you?" Miguel raised a concerned eyebrow.

"I'll be fine; I'll be behind iron bars. I'm guessing I can't get much safer for now. Besides, if I need you I'll call."

Jack watched Miguel grab Lina's arm supportively, while extending his other arm to Sam. *There's something about that angel. When he smiles, the whole world just wants to smile with him.*

As if on cue, Ed Trattoria increased the firmness of his grip on Jack to provide her direction. "What happened to your friends?"

"I don't know. What happened to them?" Jack played stupid, knowing full well where the direction of his questioning was going.

"I would have thought that they would stay to help you."

"The guilty need help," Jack pursed her lips. "This was a genuine misunderstanding. I'll be just fine. You have the money and you did say it was just protocol. Is there something else I should be concerned about?"

"Huh," Ed raised his eyebrows in apparent confusion.

"Then perhaps you would be kind enough to give me a quiet cell." Jack stared at Ed who didn't look any less confused. "You are taking me back to holding, right?"

"Yes."

"Then the least you can do is put me in a quiet cell, away from the general riff-raff.

Ed paused at the hallway intersection in response to her request. Jack sighed as the bustle of the station faded away and the hallways became more sterile. The echo of their footsteps became the predominant noise. Jack knew she was going to isolation.

"In here."

Ed stopped in front of a guard. "I need a quiet spot for Ms. Brunson here."

The guard looked up. "She a problem?"

Jack smiled at him sweetly.

Ed looked at her, "No she just doesn't belong here. So I don't want her to have to deal with the gen-pop, if she doesn't have to."

The guard looked down at his manifest. "Only got one in there. Now that one is a problem, but she's been out for a minute."

Ed pulled Jack aside. "You wanna take your chances here? I think we chock full to the brim."

"Unless you tell me you have a free interrogation room, I guess I'll take my chances here." Jack wondered how much of a problem the prisoner was. She stared at Ed's slicked-back brown hair. What had she seen in him? Her thoughts flew to Alex's smile, the twinkle in his eyes, his tousled brown hair framing his face. Then to Miguel, a polar opposite with his spiky platinum hair, often stony faced, broken only by the smile reserved for her. She couldn't contain the smile that crept across her face at the thought of the warmth of Miguel's smile.

"I hope you are taking this seriously, Jack?"

She looked into Ed's brown eyes, her smile fading fast. "Let's get on with it."

The iron bars grated as the cell door rolled into place. Jack made her way to the back of the cell and slid down the cold graffiti laden wall, to the floor. She wondered how the walls had so much writing on them when the accused were supposed to have been searched and removed of all belongings. A snort from a large, ominous woman who lay on the bench drew her attention. Jack couldn't tell if she was sleeping, but decided to keep her eye on her just in case she was really as much of a problem as the guard had indicated.

Her eyes rolled over her new surroundings, taking in the sparse furnishings, the peeling paint, and the faded graffiti. *Ed Trattoria you are being such an ass. I can't believe that you are waiting for Alex's check to clear before you release me. I can't believe that there was anything ever between us. This so sucks. Parking tickets? Some good I'm doing to the world now as mediator stuck in a jail cell. Ugh!* She hung her head in her hands in disbelief that she was even in such a predicament.

The smell of rotten eggs permeated the air. Jack cast a disgusted look over at the woman on the bench.

"You bitch; did you stink up the place?"

Jack flinched at the grating voice that broke the silence.

The woman had woken and was glaring at her. She negated the question by shaking her head.

A loud belch caused them to look upwards. A dhjinn stood in front of the camera belching. Jack heard the longest burp, which resulted in a puff of black cloud that landed on the camera's lens overhead and a shriek of laughter. It somersaulted, happy with its achievement.

"What the fuck is that?" the woman sat up, rubbing her eyes.

"You see something?" Jack asked curiously. She was happy to see the djhinn and amazed that she wasn't the only one who could see it.

"Don't you fucking see something?" the woman glared at her. "Like a large red hairy firefly with legs and on fire or something."

Jack shrugged her shoulders, smiled to the dhjinn, who was surrounded by a red pulsating flame.

It walked up to the woman, or rather it would have been walking if it hadn't been in mid-air, and stuck its tongue out. She got up from the bench. "Don't you sass me, you little shit. I'll squash you between my fingers firefly!"

Jack watched as she moved towards the Dhjinn, it moved backwards until the woman's face was squashed between the bars and her outstretched arms beyond them flailing in her attempts to snare it. The dhjinn took hold of her hair on either side of her face laughing hysterically, while it tugged each time banging the woman's head into the bars.

Jack jumped up horrified. "Stop that!"

The dhjinn let her go. Its ears and tail drooped, and it looked from under its brows like a scolded child. The disoriented woman stumbled, falling to the floor hitting her head on the concrete.

The dhjinn flitted forward then backwards, as if trying to discern whether it was in good favor, or if the woman hitting her head was its fault, too.

The doors at the end of the hallway opened and the guard rushed in with another police officer as backup. They stopped in front of the cell and stared at the woman on the floor. "What happened to her?" one asked.

Jack shrugged her shoulders nonchalantly and caught sight of the dhjinn was making sleeping signs.

"She's sleeping?" Jack offered with hesitation.

"What was that noise?" the other officer asked.

Jack raised her eyebrows, "What noise?"

"You didn't hear anything?" the officer looked at his colleague.

"Nope," Jack rubbed her palms on her bottom as she slid her hands into her back pockets.

The officers looked around and then at each other. Not seeing anything suspicious, they left.

"You might have hurt her." Jack said rushing to the woman's side, jamming her two fingers in the woman's neck quite satisfied feeling a pulse. She held out her hand, happy to see the little dhjinn. The familiar face was comforting.

It landed on her hand grinning then burst into flames, as it flew onto her other hand, dousing itself just before bringing up the other hand rubbing its body.

"Oh, you're the source of the rotten egg smell. You want to be petted. You're like a little cat, aren't you?"

The dhjinn shook its head, yes then no, not understanding the rhetorical question and changed into a little smoky dragon.

"You're a dragon?" Jack whispered in disbelief.

The fayerie cocked its head to the side, like a dog querying a high pitched sound.

The door at the end of the hallway opened. Heels could be heard clicking on the floor coming towards her at a harried and uneven pace.

CHAPTER FOURTEEN

Alex roared in pain as the surgeon rummaged around in his back with metal forceps. Finally, he extracted the trophy slug. The moment the metal object was removed; Alex's skin began regenerating. He turned to the surgeon, hissing with his fangs bared. "You'd better hurry up and be more careful Doc, my patience is wearing thin. Augy, I thought you said this guy was good."

"He is boss. Did you leave any bullets for Davern to clean up, or did you catch them all yourself?" Augy grinned at his scowling boss, motioning the doctor to continue.

"Where'd you find this one?"

"I met Dr. Ferguson at a local bar here in Russia. He's a shifter. He got mugged and shot in the States. As a human, the shot would've been fatal. As a shifter, it wasn't anything he couldn't recover from, obviously. But that meant he was forced to leave as there were witnesses that saw him get shot. He ended up in Russia staying with his mother's family for safekeeping."

Max called from across the room. He was at the computer, his fingers flying over the keys, looking like a blur.

"Damn," Augy looked at Max, "that's just unnatural."

Alex turned, scowling at the doctor. "That's where you are wrong, he's an absolute natural."

Max came over to them grinning. "I've figured it out, Dad. I know who the leak is."

Alex watched Max stroll over looking pretty pleased. He gripped onto some paper with what looked like chicken scratch mauled over it. Alex noted the many glances Max threw in the doctor's direction while inhaling his scent. He knew Max smelled the doctor's blood over the tray full of vampire blood coated slugs. Alex knew, too, that it was the doctor's blood that sparked the hunger within Max, based on the hungry look displayed on his face. His son was feeling the blood coursing through the doctor as if it were in his own body.

The doctor stopped in the middle of extracting a slug to whisper in Alex's ear, "If I have to, I would willingly donate, but I do not want to be jumped."

"Shake it off, son." Alex said to Max, who had a savage look in his eyes. "What do you have?"

"You can talk in front of Doc here. He is ours."

Augy cocked his head. Alex smiled as they both watched Max roll back his shoulders in the same manner that Alex would, to rid himself of the feeling.

"I tapped into our New York system and ran through our surveillance from the day that Jack flew from London, through to yesterday. I've seen three people with suspicious activity: Mrs. Bohmstein, Mr. Brown, or Brownie, as we all call him and a cleaning or facilities guy. Bohmstien made three calls after you contacted her. One to the airlines, one to transportation, and one to Brown; Brown also received a call from known sub-terra ally. The call lasted five minutes. Bohmstein has also been getting calls from numbers that are known to be linked with the Chinese contingency."

"Bohmstein? Are you sure, Mosquito?" Augy stared at Max with questions written all over his face. I can't believe that the little old broad could ever be up to no good.

"I know what I saw."

"Easy, Son, I don't know that we disbelieve you exactly." Alex heard Max growl at the reference to a mosquito and the doubt in his ability. He knew his son always hated being looked down upon as the little kid. Max's eyes blackened at the onset of anger, his incisors dropped at the fire that sparked an arson's glory. "I believe it is just that we are in disbelief that Bohmstein would ever betray us." Alex smiled sadly. Regardless of his love for people, this instance being one of the reasons that he trusted very few humans. He had lived over two thousand years, and always found that those close to him had been used either as a path of betrayal, or they had betrayed him by choice.

"Let the doc finish up here and we'll lock 'em and rock 'em." Alex motioned to Dr. Ferguson to wrap it up. "Max, I need to figure out who's with us and who's not. Please make that happen quickly."

Max nodded and returned to the computer.

Alex allowed Dr. Ferguson to continue plucking out the slugs from his body. The men sat in silence, listening to the noise from Max's fingers flying over the keyboard and the occasional clink of a slug being placed on a metal tray, along with the squishing sounds of flesh being cut and manipulated. This relative silence was broken by the sound of Alex's cell phone.

He cast glances at Augy and Max before answering. "Macedo here."

"Is everything okay?" Alex jumped off the table causing Dr. Ferguson's scalpel to slice his chest. Blood beaded, threatening to erupt from the seam. Ferguson threw his hands up in the air in despair.

"Keep them out of the tower until I call you, okay."

Alex closed the phone, thoughts raced through his head wondering how to use the new circumstances to his advantage.

"Everything okay, boss?"

"That was Blondie. Jack's in jail and something happened to Lina; Miguel had to take her out of the police station." Alex hated women being held in captivity, but wondered if she wasn't safer at the police station until their threat had been eliminated. "And to top it off the tower has been infiltrated. Max, I want an update," he bellowed, pushing aside Dr. Ferguson.

Alex noted that the good doctor had begun cleaning up during Max's explanation of his findings. Alex held his hand up for silence. He began to pace placing his finger on his lip. Moments passed before he spun around to face Dr. Ferguson, "You'll not be leaving us so soon, Doc."

"My job is done, sir," Dr. Ferguson bowed.

"It has been a while since I've had a doctor on staff. Perhaps you should stay," Alex smiled extending his hand.

Augy and Max stared at each other.

Alex smiled watching a sense of quiet settle over the doctor. He blinked twice running a dry tongue over his lips; Alex knew then that Dr. Ferguson had never heard or been called to the voice of a Master Vampire. He maintained eye contact with him until he felt his hand in his own.

"You okay, Doc?" Augy queried, raising an eyebrow when he seem unable to find his voice.

"Don't worry Augy, Dr. Ferguson is just fine. Aren't you? He is a little lost right now. He'll be just fine once he has committed to helping us." Alex smiled. A hint of fang glimpsed through the smile that added a modicum of warmth to his otherwise cold face.

Augy cleared his throat nervously, "Boss, he's a good guy. I cleared him..." Augy's voice trailed off, as he felt Alex power roll over him like a wave, reminding him of his place. "I'm sorry boss," Augy stuttered clutching his throat.

Max's eyes were wild. Alex could smell fear rolling off him in waves. Feeling the power of a Master vampire could be overwhelming to a fledgling, he would have to hold on.

Alex motioned to the doctor, beckoning him forward with the same sinister grin on his face.

He watched Dr. Ferguson extending his other hand to him. As he neared him, confusion turned to fear. The doctor's eyes dilated, his eyebrows furrowed, and his mouth moved frantically without sound. Alex could feel the fear rolling off him. He took a deep breath, inhaling the fear and confusion, "You are scared Doctor, I can help you. You have been quite lost; I can give you a home."

Dr. Ferguson nodded his head; his eyes never leaving Alex's face.

Alex cupped his face with as he circled him, "Do I offer what you want?"

"Who are you?" Dr. Ferguson whispered. "How do you know what I need M-Master?" He knelt at Alex's feet stuttering, staring upwards into Alex's face.

"I confess that much time has passed since I have called anyone to serve; I think the time is right now. What do you think good doctor?" Alex ran his fingers around his chin, as he stalked around to the other side of the kneeling man.

The doctor gave the barest of nods.

"Very good," Alex bent down pulling the doctor upwards and to him by his chin, exposing the carotid artery. The mesmerizing pulse beat furiously beneath the skin, as fear possessed the doctor's body. Alex smiled as he battled his control that rode the doctor's fear, incensing his hunger, threatening to tip the scales of balance. "You will take this blood oath binding yourself to me, good doctor."

He nodded feebly. His eyes closed, fluttering, as if intoxicated. Ferguson cocked his head gasping as Alex's fangs sunk deep into his neck, piercing the artery. A thick viscous sweetness flooded Alex's mouth, as Ferguson's memories unfolded. Alex felt the rejection of being forcibly exiled from New York by the lycan community after suffering a trauma that no human could survive. He felt the pain and loneliness that consumed him in solitary, he knew that Ferguson now drank too much and slept too little, looking for a solution at the bottom of the vodka glass. Alex licked his tongue over the puncture wounds, using his saliva to heal and close the bite site.

"Change my cat," Alex commanded.

Dr. Ferguson dropped on his hands and knees. His back arched, splitting his shirt in half. A scream echoed around the room as the skin undulated over the doctor's back. Bones shifted, moving under the skin's surface like tectonic plates. Skin became pelt and talons from his hind paws raged through his shoes, where simple digits had been. His spine rippled like a snapping whip, extending into a tail. The doctor's head raised upwards in a hoarse scream that became a roar, as his canines dropped into his mouth. His jaw elongated. His hazel eyes mellowed into a cool cornflower blue. With the transformation complete, Doctor Ferguson shook himself, freeing his beautiful fur from any metaphysical constraints.

"A truly magnificent Siberian White Tiger. Complete the rite, your blood with my blood to seal the oath." Alex extended a talon from an index finger, and drove it into his wrist. A thin line of blood welled up. Alex placed it in front of the tiger. The doctor blinked his cat form eyes, inhaling the scent of Alex from the line of blood at his wrist. He took a step forward and hung his head momentarily, before running his long raspy tongue over the length of Alex's arm. Once the blood was taken, he lay at Alex's feet in a submissive position.

"Good, it has been done!" Alex exclaimed. "Come as you are Doc we go to the weapons room. Max, brief us on the way down. Augy, should the good doc decide he wishes to shift back immediately, get him some clothes."

Alex set off at a good pace to the weapons room. Ferguson followed behind in full form, with Max as a close second doing his best to brief the team, though not quite sure that anyone was listening; Augy trailed. He was still shaking his head. He had seen Alex do a great many things, but control of another species was a new one for him.

CHAPTER FIFTEEN

"Oh, there you are Jack," Mrs. Stanfield stood in front of the jail cell and stuck her hands through the bars. The dhjinn dematerialized, a slight trail of smoke, the only sign of its presence. Jack got up and took her hands in greeting, not quite wanting an embrace.

"Hi Mrs. Stanfield, how are you doing?" Jack asked.

"My dear, it seems that I should be asking that of you. You poor thing. You would think that these police would have much more heinous crimes to solve rather than lock up a sweet child like you." Mrs. Stanfield looked around at the conditions in the cell and cast a dubious glance at Jack's sleeping cell mate. "Is there anything that I can do dear? Where are your friends?"

Jack smiled at the elderly lady, moved by her compassion. She gave her hands a little squeeze in appreciation. "I'll be fine, Mrs. Stanfield, thank you. It really looks worse than it is. It's just police protocol; I'll be out in the morning. Sam, Lina, and Miguel went to Sam's place. There was no point in them staying here."

"Oh alright dear, and Max?" Mrs. Stanfield's voice dropped to a whisper. She withdrew her hands from Jack's and it was clear that she had stiffened ever so slightly. Her smile was controlled. As if on cue, the scent of smoke increased.

Jack kept her voice light and moved to position herself between Mrs. Standfield and the last place she had seen the dhjinn. "Oh Max went with A… Lex… Mr. Macedo," Jack wondered what name Mrs. Stanfield knew Alex by. The world knew him as Lex Macedo, CEO of Macedo Inc., friends called him Alex, and strangers got some other alias usually a derivation of Alexander, his birth given name. Jack decided that Lex would be the most appropriate fit, given the circumstances.

"Oh, I see. Okay dear. Well, I suppose I must be going if I can't be of any help here. I need to get in touch with Max. If you hear from him before I do, would you mind asking him to give me a call?" Mrs. Stanfield smiled again; a smile that barely left her mouth and didn't warm her face or touch her eyes. It was not genuine. She touched the metal bars fleetingly, as if leaving were awkward.

The sound of her heels clicking over the floor was just as harried and uneven on her exit as it was her entrance.

Jack turned around to find the dhjinn staring at her. It had its arms crossed and was pouting. "Listen my little dragon friend. I'm not sure how you got here; I need to know if you can find my friends. I need to make sure they are okay. Can you do that for me?" Jack looked into its red eyes. The little creature stared back lovingly, nodding its head, yes. It had been considered a friend, a great honor.

"Okay, find Miguel and Sam. I'm not worried about Lina, just Miguel and Sam. Do you know who they are?"

The dhjinn changed its head to represent a small Lina, Alex, Sam, Max, and finally Miguel. Jack picked the representations that she wanted.

"Can you find them?" Jack asked again.

The dhjinn imaged Miguel's head before holding her nose between its fingers.

"He smells bad?" Jack mused, "That's what Alex and Lina say. Hurry back little friend."

****

"There's nothing much here in the form of weaponry," Alex looked around the room disapprovingly. "We'll have to go to the tower."

"How are we going to get there? You're can't carry us all." Augy looked around the room and at Dr. Ferguson, who lay at Alex's feet, panting.

"Portal," Max's eyes lit up. "We can open a portal."

Alex was mildly amused at Max's excitement. "Can you do that?"

"I think so. I remember everything that my mother used to do."

Still amused, Alex watched as Max looked around the armory searching for something. He found a sharpie.

"This'll have to do."

Alex returned Max's grin and waved him onwards. Max went to the wall and drew a doorway; he closed his eyes and Alex couldn't help but raise his eyebrows when Max mumbled some words. When he reopened his eyes they were glowing gold, and he had a satisfied smile on his face. He stuck his head through the doorway. "I did it." He turned smiling at everyone.

"You dropped them."

"Dropped what?" Max looked at Augy, who dropped his fangs.

"Oh, sorry. I guess I got a little excited and didn't notice."

The team hurried through the portal which put them in Alex's bedroom. Alex moved to his walk-in closet and the team followed him. He parted his suits at the back and slid the false wall backwards, exposing a door that looked as if it could have been hiding Fort Knox. Alex placed his hand on the palm reader and a sensor sprung up, piercing his hand, barely missing all the bones. Alex clenched his teeth, controlling his body's responses to the pain.

"Access granted Alexander." A simulated voice surrounded them. The vault door slid open, exposing a stairway that mysteriously lit itself. Alex led the way down the stairwell and through a hallway that ended abruptly.

Alex looked at the group's confused faces. Bracing himself against the wall, he pushed on the left side. The sound of stone grating on stone echoed throughout the hallway, as Alex strained. The giant wall shifted, sliding until there was just enough room for them to pass.

Once behind the wall, they entered a room that held all types of paraphernalia. A wide array of ancient texts sat gathering dust on a bookshelf. Ancient chests with contained mysteries were stacked in a corner. Paintings and tapestries adorned one wall, the excess leaned against another.

Alex turned to Max and Augy, their mouths agape as they absorbed his secret collection of artifacts. Even Dr. Ferguson in his Siberian Tiger form was enthralled. "Snap out of it people. We have no time for a tour." He called Max and Augy's attention to the far wall where he stood. "Suit up. Find a weapon of choice. We are going to clean house."

Alex put on a full length trench coat that matched the material of his pants and shirt. The material fluidly followed his every movement; he looked like running water in motion. He finished buckling his holster straps and reached for his sabre, which sung as the blade slid along the table top. To finish off, he tucked his Sig Sauer into its holster under his right arm.

"Max, you are going to the top of the tower to be the eyes and ears of the operation. You know who we're are going after and you'll be able to find them. I want limited liabilities on this one. We will have a small window of opportunity. Have Davern on standby. As we are ready to rock and roll, send the building into lockdown, this will alert the fire department and call for an evacuation of the building by floor. We will have fifteen minutes to eliminate all targets."

He heard Augy chuckled from across the room at Max, who raised his hands up with his gun selection in hand. "You have chosen wisely, Mosquito."

"Why do you keep calling me that?" Max growled, his humor waning.

"Even the gun you have selected has your name sake?"

"What?"

"You have selected a Sig Mosquito," Augy was laughing again and Alex joined him this time.

"Aww, no way," Max checked the gun's barrel. "What are the odds?" he began laughing, too. "Well, hopefully we'll do each other some good. Guns aren't my thing."

The three vampires sealed off the vault and jogged back along the corridor, this time turning off along the tunnel that led up to the Macedo Tower. At the parking lot, the team made their way to the elevator, using the shadows and stealth to their advantage, even the large Siberian Tiger was barely noticeable.

The elevator groaned under the weight of the four beings. Alex peeked over Max's shoulder as he plugged his phone into the elevator's circuit panel, tapping into his network to validate the security of the penthouse suite.

"We're clear," he mumbled, as he continued tapping the buttons, sending the elevator upwards.

Once in the penthouse, Max jumped over the balcony landing in his living room. He glanced upwards at Alex. "Cool. I've always wanted to do that without hurting myself." Before he could be reprimanded from Alex, he ran off to his office sliding into his chair. He activated the panels; fingers flying over the keys with the barest of touches. Images flew over the six monitors as Max scanned the penthouse until he found what he was looking for.

"I have them," he called.

Let's try a little covertness Max. Use your thoughts to communicate with us until all is resolved. Alex pressed his thoughts into Max's mind.

Max followed Alex's thought trail. *Whoa! Instant intercom. I like it. Man this new body has awesome perks.*

Max focus.

Sorry, okay. I have three on the fifteenth in the data archive, another three on the fifth and three more heading to your office on the first floor.

Alex, Augy and Doc stepped back onto the groaning elevator as they descended to floor fifteen. *Aug – I smell them. They are in the back, left corner.*

Yeah, boss, I got them.

They split up. The room housed computing equipment which was laid out in rows. It was freezing but neither Alex's and Augy's skin nor the thick pelt of the tiger was affected; cold air blew upwards with force through the tiny holes in the raised flooring. Each being stalked an infiltrator down a computer row heading towards the far left corner of the room.

As they approached, Alex could see that the infiltrators were plugged into the network. Cables and wires were piggybacked off of wires leading back to a laptop precariously poised on top of a monitor. With all his limited knowledge of technology even Alex could see that they were extracting information onto portable hardware.

Max, they look like they are taking information?

Yeah, they cracked my infrastructure and have gotten to a few things.

What were they after?

They appear to have targeted financial data and have been trying to crack an archive named Leonides.

I thought you told me that the network was impenetrable.

That was from the outside. I never thought that I would have to protect us from within.

Sounds like you have a pet project coming down the pike.

Alex's last thought came out with a grunt, as he lunged at the vampire intently focused on the monitor. In a single movement Alex appeared behind the vamp whispering in his ear. "I hope you found what you were looking for." Without waiting for an answer, Alex severed the vamp's head.

Augy wrestled his vamp without much of a scuffle, driving his hand through the vamp's chest and squashing his heart. The third vamp was hiding a little further away from the other two, in a more distant aisle, perhaps in the capacity of a lookout. He was no match for Alex's and Augy's speed. He was much too young of a vamp to stand up against either of them. As he backed down the aisle, he didn't notice the large Siberian Tiger blocking his exit behind him, at least not until he fell on top of him. The doc made little time slitting his throat with a swift paw movement. He couldn't incapacitate the vamp fully in his form.

Sir, I can't take this one's head, but he has been incapacitated for now. The doctor called to Alex.

The team had made quick work of the intruders on the fifteenth floor. Alex pressed the young inexperienced vamp for information which he relinquished readily before Alex expired him. The fifth floor was no different and the team was just heading into the first floor when Max called out.

Wait.

What is it Max? Alex cautiously stepped back into the shadows.

Blondie has just entered into your office. He has a gun and has it pointed at Bohmstein. But Brownie also just entered the scene from the other side. He has his gun pointed at Blondie. There are three other vamps. I don't think that Blondie knows they are there. He is outnumbered.

Not anymore Max, not anymore.

CHAPTER SIXTEEN

"Talk to me, talk to me," Alex checked his face in the mirror one last time talking out loud, while he also sent his mental messages.

Boss, I got Bohmstein and Brownie subterra… Blondie is there too; he's not looking good. Augy's voice made a mental impression.

Aug, get the truth and then have the doctor fix him up.

Dad, Max's voice came to him firmly.

What's up, son?

That cop is almost at Macedo Inc. front doors. We are not quite clear. Davern has one more floor to take care of. Can you stall him?

How long do you need?

Ten minutes?

I'm in my quarters I'll stall the cop but tell Davern to get it wrapped up in five. Alex slicked back his hair and imaged some stubble and a faint mustache.

On it.

Max's words faded as Alex left his apartment and strode to greet the police and fire fighters at the front doors. They were responding to the alarms. He bulked up a little with every step preparing to play the role of Lex Macedo.

By the time he reached the front door, Alex's permagrin had already taken residence on his face.

"Good evening officers and fire fighters. Thank you for responding so quickly, but I fear we may have had a building software glitch. We are unable to locate the fire that the alarms identified." Alex spoke through the glass doors, as he signaled the security guard to unlock the doors to let them in.

Ed Trattoria was the first one through the door. He eyed Alex suspiciously, taking the status of the environment. The building had been evacuated with the exception for security. "Everyone is outside?"

"Hmm, yes Detective, our protocols require evacuation for the safety of our personnel." Alex gave Ed his best smile.

"Software glitch, huh? The department will still need to check things out." Alex watched Ed motioned to the fire department to enter the building, begrudgingly he acknowledged Alex's welcoming arms.

"Well, Detective," Alex was sure to emphasize the first syllable. He followed up with his best Lex Macedo smile "We are not sure if we've had an infrastructure intrusion. I have my analysts working on the issue. If we determine this to be the case, I may need to file a report."

"Have we met?" Ed stared quizzically into Alex's eyes.

"Oh Detective, the possibilities are endless. I attend many local events. I'm sure our circles may have crossed multiple times. I apologize if I don't recall your name," Alex extended his hand with seeming warmth. "Lex Macedo."

"I know who you are," a puzzled look still dominated Ed's face. He reached slowly for Alex's hand. "Edward Trattoria."

Ed's voice trailed off as Alex whirled around to face the security guard at the front desk. He stared momentarily at his hand left hanging in the air, and Alex's retreating figure.

Alex threw an apology over his shoulder as he headed to the front desk.

"Macedo," Alex answered the phone gruffly.

"We're clean," Max's voice filtered over the phone.

"Excellent. Good work." Alex turned to give Ed a smile.

"Dad, we have another problem."

"What's that?"

"I can't get hold of Sam."

"Should we be worried?" Alex knitted his brows trying to feel for Sam and Jack, but finding only Jack.

"I think so. I can't feel her anymore. Something is wrong." Max was clearly worried.

"Okay, relax. We'll handle it and I'm sure all will work itself out." Alex hung up the phone; not without sending Max a mental note letting him know that he would stop by Sam's apartment after he picked up Jack from the police station. Alex could smell Ed standing right behind him, but spun around in surprise anyway.

"Detective, I didn't realize you were right behind me." Alex tried to sound surprised. He hoped it didn't come out a bit tired.

"Is all okay in the Macedo world?" Ed asked, shifting his weight from one foot to the other.

"Hmm," Alex pondered on what story to lead him with. "Well, I'm not sure. Perhaps you can help me. My brother tells me that a friend of his is in your jail because you are waiting for my check to clear. And someone potentially has hacked into my network. Which one of these issues can you help me with today?" Alex raised an eyebrow in query. "Is my money no longer good enough for the city of New York?"

"Oh, no sir. I cannot go into details. The department protocol serves that we wait until the check clears before we release anyone." Ed shifted his weight again under Alex's stare. "Your brother, would that be one, Xan Macedo?"

"Hmm, do you know him?"

"Not really sir, only through a friend."

"I want you to arrange for her release. Otherwise, I'll be rescinding my donation to the department. Have a good day Detective," Alex emphasized the first syllable in Detective.

****

"Yes, sir," Ed straightened himself calling after Alex's rapidly retreating figure. He slapped himself in the forehead. "Yes sir? Yes sir? Damn what was I thinking?" Ed grumbled out loud. He caught the security guard's eyes. "What are you looking at?"

"Don't worry, he has that effect with everyone," the guard offered.

"Great," Ed mumbled and slumped out the door waiting for the fire fighters to give the all clear. He pulled out his cell phone to make a few calls, while he waited for the firefighters to give the all clear.

CHAPTER SEVENTEEN

"Sir, sir, you can't go in there," the pleading frantic voice trailed after Alex, as he strode down the hall to Jack's cell.

"Jack, honey, are you okay?" Alex's titanium grey eyes scanned her for signs of injury. Worry lines marked his brows.

Jack couldn't help but smile. The excessive waiting had been tiring. "Yes, Alex, I'm fine. I just need to get outta here." She accepted his embrace through the bars enjoying his concern.

Alex beckoned the guard who was hurrying down the hallway. Once the doors opened, Alex drew her into his arms until he felt Jack squirm a little. "I was worried," he explained.

"I know," Jack eased out of his arms, only to find herself being ushered out of the police station into Alex's waiting limo.

"Alex, is there something else going on? It was just parking tickets?" Jack tried to read his well-guarded face. "Where are we going?" she glanced out the window at the diminishing police station, not at all sorry to see it go.

Alex's hand swept under her hair to cup her jaw, his fingertips lightly touched the length of her neck, pulling her into him. His eyes stared into the emerald depths of hers. After a moment, he found the yielding softness that he was looking for, and his lips brushed hers. Firm, yet tender.

"Alex, what's wrong?" Jack managed to whisper.

Alex's lips moved against her neck. "My empire is under attack. My family is under attack, and the best way that I found to protect you was to leave you in the custody of the police."

"It's fine Alex. I was okay" Jack leaned into Alex's caresses until the faint wisp of rotten eggs passed her nose. She felt Alex stiffen, as he scented the air.

As soon as Jack saw the fireball begin to form, she grabbed and stuffed it into her pocket.

"What was that all about?"

"Umm, are you okay with dragon fayeries?"

"What?" Alex looked quite confused, almost as if he had just heard of a new species.

Jack looked at him from under her eyebrows. "Well you were the one that said you couldn't be around the fayerie," Jack released the little fireball that was in rare form.

The dhjinn waggled its finger at Jack for being stuffed into a pocket.

Alex was in fits of laughter.

Jack reminded the dhjinn that it had jumped into her pocket on its own accord the last time.

"It's a dhjinn they are slightly different than fayerie," Alex said once his bouts of laughter subsided, "and yeah, I'm okay."

"Whatever," Jack glared at him.

"Try offering her a peace offering," Alex suggested.

"Like what?"

Alex smiled. Reaching over, he deftly plucked a shell button off of Jack's silk shirt, causing it to bare more of her bosom than she was comfortable with.

The dhjinn was quite pleased with the peace offering. It banged the button against its head several times, and polished it, looking at its warped mother-of-pearl reflection; it even tried biting, but decided that the taste wasn't good.

Jack was caught up in the moment, laughing at its antics. A distant siren brought her back to her senses. "Alex, where are we going?"

He stroked a stray hair from Jack's face. "Sam's flat. Max thinks something is wrong. I told him I'd check it out."

"Alex, I had asked the dragon to go to Sam's house earlier. I wonder if she saw anything, or anyone."

The dhjinn nodded its head vigorously imaging Lina and Miguel, one after the other, wrapping its arms around itself to show them in an embrace, and then disappeared.

Alex pursed his lips acknowledging Lina and Miguel in yet another seeming embrace.

Jack leaned forward staring into the space where the dhjinn was. "She's gone."

"Maybe that's what Lina and Miguel did after they embraced," Alex mused.

The dhjinn reappeared pointing to her nose laughing.

Jack leaned back into the plush leather of the limo. "What about Sam?"

The dhjinn froze, her ears drooped and she became sad. She looked at Jack with large sorrowful eyes. "The scary lady took her away in a prison."

"Which scary lady?" Jack asked

Jack saw Mrs. Stanfield's head floating on its body.

"Stanfield," Alex was also staring at the floating head.

"She stopped by the jail and asked how I was doing. I told her where Sam was. Oh my God!" Jack looked upwards. "Oops, sorry."

"Why was she looking for Sam?" "I think she was looking for Max more than she was looking for Sam."

"Hmm. Something is not adding up."

The limo came to a stop.

"Do you have a spare gun in here?" Jack was looking through the compartments in the limo.

"I don't use guns unless I absolutely have to and even then, I don't keep them lying around for anyone to casually borrow." Alex shrugged his shoulders as he got out of the limo. He didn't want to tell her that he had just put his Sig Sauer back into his armory at the Tower. "Are you coming?"

****

Jack sank back into the plush leather seat, rolling her eyes upwards, before mustering her resolve to jettison through the open limo door, into the orange glow of the high pressure sodium lighting.

Once on the sidewalk, she checked both directions on the street. For good measure, she glanced upwards. Her years as a private detective told her to check the street for oncoming trouble; her recent experience as the earth's Peace Keeper, warned her that if trouble were going to come, it would come from all directions.

Alex was nowhere in sight, she walked up the stairs and reached for the door. It was opened.

"Sam," Jack called as she looked around.

"No," Alex's face was grim. "It's just me."

"Is Sam here?"

"No."

"Any signs of where she might be?"

"Not that I can see."

"C'mon upstairs, there's something you might want to see."

Jack followed him up the stairs to Sam's second floor New York two-story apartment. As she climbed, Sam's high-pitched giggle filtered through her memories. Jack's fingers trailed over the textured wallpaper that lined the stairwell as she ascended.

"Don't worry, we'll find her."

Jack looked up to find Alex's reassuring smile. "I know Alex, I know." Taking a deep breath at the top of the stairs, Jack scanned the room. "So what did you find?"

"This way," Alex pointed upwards.

"More stairs?"

At the top, she found herself in the midst of a loft style bedroom. The ceiling-to-floor windows were lined with black heavy velvet drapery. She smiled, thinking that it had been a while since Sam actually stayed here. The drapes held a thin layer of dust. Earth tones decorated the room, Jack felt as if she'd just walked into the fall season. The room felt warm and welcoming, until something crunched under her foot. Looking down, she gasped. A wax candle lay broken under her foot, one candle of five that still remained standing.

The wolf tattoo uncurled across her back.

"Shh," Jack whispered to it, as she stared at the pentagram engraved into the floorboards with a candle at each point.

"What?" Alex queried.

"Not you," Jack quipped.

"Then who?" Alex raised an eyebrow

Figuring he wouldn't understand, Jack redirected. "Can you smell anything?"

"Jack, how many times have I told you, I'm not a blood hound," Alex retorted.

"I know," she hurried over the window where Alex stood staring out. Leading him back to the pentagram, she said,

"Can't you try? Sometimes you are able to smell or sense things?"

Jack watched the brief smile flit across his face. She breathed a sigh of relief as she saw him relax. His head bowed close to her, as she looked at him. Jack found herself breathing in his essence and losing herself in her want for him. Her head tilted, as her lips moved towards his.

****

"Lina," Alex jerked his head upwards exhaling sharply, "Miguel."

Alex caught Jack as she stumbled backwards. He noted the expression on her face, but couldn't quite discern if it were one of surprise or shock. "Are you okay?"

"Yes, I'm fine."

Alex noted her recovery from whatever surprised her, was quick.

"What about Lina or Miguel? Are those the only scents you picked up?" Jack pressed.

"No, they aren't the only ones, Sam's scent is strong; that's not surprising as this is her place. I also picked up a whiff of the Stanfield witch and Lina's scent intermingled with Miguel's." Alex mused as he recollected. Turning back to Jack, he said, "I want you to go back to Macedo Tower and wait with Augy. I have to make a quick trip."

"Okay."

Alex thought about ignoring all of the questions in Jack's eyes, but then again he didn't want her going off on some half-baked mission on her own. "I'm going to make a trip downstairs", he said pointing downward. "I want to see her father and just make sure that nothing is brewing."

"Oh my goodness," Jack breathed. "I hadn't thought of that." She patted her pockets getting ready to leave.

"Oh and Jack—"

"What's up?" Jack spun around to face him.

He wondered why her face was blank. She was definitely hiding something. No time to find out now. "Stay away from Max. He's not ready to be alone with anyone. No matter how familiar everything looks. Make sure Augy is with you at all times."

"Okay."

Alex placed his hand on his hip with mild annoyance. "Don't take this lightly, Jack. I'm serious. I'm counting on you to keep yourself safe for a few hours."

"Okay. Okay." Jack nodded and trotted off down the stairs.

Alex listened, following her footsteps to the next level, out the front door and into the limo.

Moving to the window, he watched it pull away. Sighing, he scanned the bedroom. Drawn to the bed, he trailed his fingertips over the disheveled bed linens.

"Lina," he exhaled. "What is going on sweetheart? What are you not telling me?"

Before an eyelash could complete a blink, Alex was gone.

CHAPTER EIGHTEEN

Alex tapped a rift and entered the seventh level of hell, in the council chambers. Standing in the middle of the chamber floor, the power rippled over him like cool breeze on a summer day, touching every orifice on his skin, as hell welcomed him. Except this wasn't a refreshing breeze. This was pure undeniable raw power.

He flexed his muscles to maintain the control he would need to get through a round with Lina's father, the king of all evilness – Lucifer himself. The allure to lose control was eminent. Hell was alive with the blood of countless souls, trapped in the varying levels. The curdling screams could pierce his conscience and render him mad if he didn't maintain control.

Alex scanned the room acclimating himself. He snapped his fingers and the flames blazoned in the sconces, throwing the shadows of the lost souls in a motion picture across the room.

He crossed the chamber floor and vaulted over the raised semicircular dais and stone table into his chair. He smiled, as he settled into his rite, the rush of blood transferred to him immediately from the seat. After all, he was the head of the house for the sixth level of hell, a position seeded to him by Lina and the fifth level, a position won in the defeat of Xylar. It was only natural that the chair replenished him. Leaning further into the chair, he cocked his feet up onto the council table.

Closing his eyes, he ran his senses along hell's blood, searching for answers like a hacker infiltrating a new computer network. It would only be a matter of time before his presence was found.

Alex didn't have to wait long. His eyes flew open at the oncoming clattering of hooves on the stone floor. Closing his eyes in an air of peace, Alex settled back, waiting for the angry entrance.

As expected, the chamber doors went flying open at the flick of Lucifer's hand motion. "What in the name of FUCK is going on?"

Alex opened an eye and sat up slowly. "Is there a problem?"

"You," Lucifer pointed at him angrily. "What are you looking for? I feel you searching, feeling along every blood line in hell."

Alex stood up with an air of laziness, casually jumping back over the table to land in front of Lucifer on the chamber floor. "Do you mean to tell me, you, the all-knowing and all-powerful King of the Underworld, have no idea what's going on." Alex squinted his eyes giving Lucifer a calculating stare.

"Careful boy, on the ground upon which you tread," Lucifer waved a loaded finger at him. A flame licked at his horned nail.

"I just cannot believe that situations manifest in hell without your knowledge or distinct approval." Alex cupped his chin in thought taking a softer position.

"Little goes on with my knowledge," Lucifer acquiesced. "Why are you here?"

"Should I have called?" Alex jibed.

"Indeed."

"Your daughter has me a bit baffled, I must admit," Alex scanned Lucifer's face for any tell-tale warning signs.

"See a marriage counselor. How so?" The daemon king responded gritting his teeth.

"Every time I encounter her, she is covered with angel dust. I'm trying to speculate upon her plan, assuming she has one."

"Is there trouble in paradise?" Lucifer grinned raising an eyebrow.

Alex growled, "Only if your daughter is bedding that angel."

Lucifer bulked up in size, Alex knew he had struck a nerve. "You are running out of get out of hell cards, boy."

"I am head of the Sixth House of Hell, seeded to me by your daughter. If she will not act like the crowned prince then I will." Alex bulked in size as well. Dark blood rushed throughout him; he controlled the anger, allowing it to push him only so far.

"You may have a point." Lucifer calmed down waving Alex backwards. "Handle your business, son. I will check up on my daughter as well. I have no knowledge of her affairs."

Alex stuck his taloned hands into the stone table and the dark blood from hell pulsated through him. After a moment, he withdrew his hand. "She's not here, and there's been no trace of her. If I have to, I'm going to go up to eight and get her."

Lucifer spun about. Horror covered his face. "You don't think she'd actually go up there willingly?"

"Not willingly. That angel took her there once and if she's there, I'll get her back." Alex growled normalizing his size, as he maintained his control over the power. "On that you have my word."

"Hmpf!"

Alex watched as Lucifer spun on his heels to make his exit, yelling in what Alex supposed was an ancient daemonic tongue.

Standing alone in the chamber, Alex relaxed, allowing his shoulder to sag. Finding determination, he tapped a rift.

CHAPTER NINETEEN

The limousine came to a halt and the driver eased around the stretch to open the door. Jack smiled into the waiting stoic face, as she exited the vehicle, accepting the chauffeur's hand. Her smile faded upon realization that it was not reciprocated. A scowl crept across her face and to her surprise, the chauffeur smiled. Jack noticed his teeth were beautiful and white. Not a hint of an elongated eyetooth anywhere.

She remembered the task at hand and strode off towards the elevator. Thankfully it was waiting.

The ride up to the penthouse seemed to move slowly as Jack pondered the day's events. Her thoughts landing on Miguel and his strange absence, finally, it lingered on Alex's closeness.

Every time I allow myself to get close to Alex, I like, lose track of everything. Jack began pacing in the elevator. *I have to admit that I do feel something for him. Damn it, he is one sexy vampire, but that's just it; he is a vampire. Undead. Cold, not living – and married. And here I am supposed to be the mediator of the universe, okay only between terra and the surrounding planes, but still, I can't make a good decision between men. Shit! They aren't even men. What am I thinking? Miguel is the Archangel of Light for the heavens. Where has he been? Some Warrior of Light when he is gallivanting around with Prince Lina. I have no idea why she is not a Princess, but anyways I have a good mind to call him right now.*

Jack looked around the elevator. *Hmm, it's kinda tight in here, for all those feathers and wings. Maybe not a good idea. Why do I get myself wrapped up in men that are so complex?*

The elevator dinged. She breathed a sigh of relief and stepped out. She was beginning to feel claustrophobic with her thoughts.

Her footsteps were quiet as she padded down the staircase to the living space. She heard voices in the office area beyond the kitchen. She trained her ear, but couldn't make out the conversation.

****

"Everything restored kid?" Augy pointed to the monitors watching the data fly over the screens.

"Yeah, they didn't get as much as I thought just a partial on that one file," Max grinned.

"I brought you a bottle of Sam's finest to top you up."

"You think I need it?" Max questioned. "I don't feel anything weird."

"Max your body is still adjusting, by the time you feel something, it is too late. So until you have regulated, it's best to eat around the clock."

"Alright, you know best."

Augy watched Max chug the bottled blood. "Easy kid, take it slow. Never rush it."

The bell from the elevator broke their attention. Augy scented the air. "It's Jack, Kid are you good?"

"I'm good."

"If you're not good, if you're not in control, you could hurt her."

Augy watched as Max took another swig from this bottle, this time slow and controlled.

"I promise Aug, I'm good."

****

"Hi Guys," Jack beamed seeing Augy and Max staring at the bank of monitors and deep in conversation.

She gasped when Max turned his head.

"Is everything okay?" he asked.

Jack peered at him. "You look amazing. Oh my goodness. You look so, I don't know, the word escapes me, maybe beautiful?" she exhaled and rushed over to embrace him. She felt him stiffen.

"I'm sorry; I know I'm usually not a hugger. I'm so happy to see you alive and well." She moved away. "I really just was…" her voice slowed as she stared at him. His eyes were becoming bloodshot. Jack noticed that he hadn't blinked once since she moved back. "…happy to see you, but then you are not alive anymore. Right." Jack paused taking a deep breath. "I'm sorry I forgot that. I'm making a mess of this aren't I?" She jutted out her chin. "Are we going to be okay?"

Augy moved behind Max and placed a hand on his shoulder. "Hello Ms. Brunson, good to see you. Everything is fine."

Jack noticed the emphasis that Augy place on his last three words and smiled.

"Hey Doc, why don't you escort Ms. Brunson to her quarters, I'm sure she may want to freshen up?"

Jack only had to wonder for a moment who Augy was talking to, when her eyes trained on movement at the back of the office. She screamed realizing a large white tiger was moving towards her, and reached for her absent gun.

Augy held up his hand signaling the tiger to stop. "Ms. Brunson, this is Dr. Ferguson. He is a shifter and the newest member of our team."

Jack's breathing was labored. "Right, of course; why wouldn't he be?"

"Doc, why don't you change, maybe something of Max will fit you?"

Jack noted that Augy's nails were now talons and digging into Max's shoulder. Max's eyes seemed normal, except he appeared to be in pain.

"Augy you're hurting him," Jack threw him a questioning stare. She gulped as her peripheral vision witnessed Dr. Ferguson shifting into human form. He sauntered off into Max's adjoining bedroom.

"Better him than you Ms. Brunson." Augy grinned. "The pain reminds him to be human."

"I'm okay, Jack," Max's voice was feeble.

"Wow, you even sound different," she stepped back.

"You're not afraid?"

"No, just giving you space," Jack managed a grin.

"Were you with Alex when he went over to Sam's? I smell her place on you. Like wafts of a spent candle."

"She wasn't there. Your mother was there though. So were Lina and Miguel."

Jack watched Augy loosen his grip on Max's shoulder.

"Alex went down there to check on things," she pointed down, "he'll be back soon then we'll figure it out." A loud crash in the living area sent her rushing out of the office to investigate. Remembering she didn't have her gun, she was glad when she was overtaken by Augy and Max. Doc was the last by her side; she was still a little unsure about him.

The air was filled with the sickening smell of burnt flesh and singed feathers.

The doctor rushed to the side of Miguel, who lay in a ball cringing from pain.

Jack moved to his side with her mouth hanging open. She could see parts of him were still burning as the doctor worked diligently to extinguish the hungry embers. His wings were gone. She blinked in disbelief. His magnificent wings were now no more than a charred bony skeleton.

Jack dropped to her knees and reached for his blistered hand. She heard the doctor barking orders for water and clean rags. As she blinked, the pandemonium faded into the background, her eyes locked with Miguel's.

"What happened?"

"He has forsaken me?"

Miguel's eyes were flat, yet Jack searched them for answers. She squeezed his hand causing them to open a little wider. "Talk to me Mig, who did this?"

"He has forsaken me?"

Jack watched as Miguel's eyes closed and his hand went limp. She reached for the doc. "Is he…"

"He has gone into stasis. Angel's don't die, but they can suffer injuries that require their bodies to go into a coma induced sleep that will allow regeneration."

Jack sighed in relief. "So what do we do now with him?"

"We need to keep him in a sterile dark room where no one can harm him. He is quite vulnerable in this stage."

"Oh crap. Great. Do we have anything big enough for him?"

"What about Dad's ice chest?" Max offered.

"That might work," Doc looked around nodding.

"Augy, so you'll figure out something for security then? And you'll all get him down there?"

"I will Ms. Brunson." Augy furrowed his brows. "Where will you be?"

"I'll be in my room. I need a moment. I'll meet you guys back in Alex's quarters. Doc, how long does this stasis thing take?"

He shrugged his shoulders. "Ma'am, I'm a shifter. I have never ever seen an angel in real life before this one. I'm only hoping everything that I heard is true, so we can help him."

"I know who I can ask." Jack made short work of getting to her room in the Macedo Tower. A ruffling of wings made her turn quickly to face Raphael the Archangel.

"I was just about to call you," Jack smiled sweetly.

"I cannot help him." Raphael's face was blank.

"Why not? Isn't he one of you? Aren't you an angel? Don't you help people? Isn't that your job?" Jack's smile was now nowhere to be found.

"I am indeed an archangel. I am a healer, but it is forbidden to help him."

"Why"

"I cannot explain."

"That forbidden too?"

Raphael smiled.

"You are infuriating right now," Jack sneered. "So why are you here if you are forbidden to function?"

"I have been assigned to you as your Angel of Light. As the Peacekeeper, you are required to have a Warrior of Light to maintain the balance."

"I have a Warrior of Light and he is hurt right now." Jack's hands found her hips. She gripped them tightly in an effort not to unleash her anger at the smiling archangel in front of her.

"If you are referring to Miguel, he is no longer your assigned Warrior."

"Since when?" Jack narrowed her eyes.

"All that matters now is that I'm here to protect you."

"I'm not feeling so good about that, Raphael. You won't even follow my direction. So can I order you to help him?"

"The order I was given will outrank your request."

"Will you at least tell me how we can help him?" Jack softened her tone. "His body was burnt badly and his glorious wings are now nothing but bones. It all looks so painful. Please find it within you to help me. I need to help him. What has he possibly done to deserve this? No one deserves this."

"There is not much you can do, but I will help you to tend to his injuries. He must find his own way home."

"Thank you, Raphael."

"Where is he?"

"I'll take you to him."

CHAPTER TWENTY

"What the fuck is going on here?" Alex's voice echoed around his apartment. He noted that Jesus, his hell hound, had been locked in his bathroom. Augy, Max, Doc, Jack, and an archangel whose wing plumage was vaguely familiar, stood huddled around his ice chest. "If you are hungry you are all on the wrong floor and in the wrong icebox," Alex growled wishing for privacy so he could think.

"Dad, any news of Sam?" Max darted forward.

"Not yet, son, but I have a feeling that all will break loose soon and we will find her." Alex attempted a smile to allay Max's concern. "How are you doing and what the fuck is going on here?"

"I'm working on it Dad, just worried about Sam." Max chucked a hitch-hiker's thumb over his shoulder. "That's Miguel, he came crashing into the penthouse all charred and burned like he'd been to hell and back. Doc says he's in some sort of stasis or coma."

"Doctor," Alex growled patting Max on his arm as he moved towards the icebox. "I need to speak with that archangel."

"He can't speak. I can't help him." Dr. Ferguson stammered. "I don't know how."

"He's right Alexander. Miguel is in a state where no one can reach him until his body and mind find balance."

"Raphael! I knew that I recognized those wings." Alex's smile was brief. "Don't hand me that horse shit. I will go and pluck the very memories that I need out of his angelic mind. Why are you here?"

"I have been assigned to the Keeper. I told her I would aid in healing his physical injuries only."

"Why not help your brother all the way back through?" Alex mused.

"I cannot."

"Because he crossed the line," Alex queried.

Raphael smiled.

"I see, well you might want to stay your help until after I'm done with him."

"You will not harm him."

"Is that an order Raphael, or a request, a suggestion even? I'm guessing that your orders were not to aid him or provide him any protection in any way. I'll also remind you that I outrank you just as I outrank him." Alex's sarcasm dominated his smile. He blazed his commands, his patience was wearing thin. "Now stand down. He was the last one of us to see both Sam and Lina and I need to know what happened to them."

Raphael took a few steps back. Alex strode towards the ice chest.

"He should remain in a sterile environment," Doc started.

Alex put up his hand silencing the doctor, who fell to his knees as Alex's power ran over him.

"Alex," Jack queried.

"He'll be fine," Alex mumbled, as he opened the ice chest. He acknowledged that Miguel looked like shit. He wondered what it would have taken for him to enter into hell and risk his own immortality. "I guess I'm going to find out," Alex grunted as he vamped out and stuck all ten of his talons into Miguel's head.

"Stay back," he roared as he heard steps advance towards him.

The light was blinding. Alex had never been inside an angel's head, let alone that of an archangel. The noise was overwhelming. Children's laughter echoed everywhere, music from the ice cream truck blared, and angelic chorus could be heard in every direction. The smell of fresh flowers infused his senses, thwarting his focus and the deafening light blinded him.

Miguel you are in this chaos somewhere. Help me and let me help you.

Alex.

Miguel is that you, your voice is weak and faint.

Alex, Lina is in trouble. The babies are in trouble.

Where are they?

I took them as far as I could to sub2.

You went two levels down? Why? Alex felt tears burning his eyes, challenging him to maintain his grip. The pain of the mind locked with the angel was almost too much to bear.

The babies were eating her from the inside. I was helping her to feed on animals, as neither the synthetic blood nor the aged blood was helping her. My Lord said he would help her, but when I took her to him, she looked like she was dying. I have never defied him, stood up to him, yes; defied him, no. I flew as fast as I could to sub2 and dropped her there where her father said he would keep her alive.

I asked my Lord for mercy and forgiveness and I got nothing. He has forsaken me.

We will deal with that later. Raphael is waiting to help heal your injuries. When he touches you, you use that energy to find your way back. You must finish that fight later, it's not over.

Why is Raphael helping me?

Jack called him. Where did you last see Sam?

The lady Stanfield was coming to Sam's place. So Sam asked Lina and I to go, seeing as the lady would last remember Lina as an exiled daemon.

Miguel, one more thing.

Alex

You are a warrior. You have defeated many across centuries and sustained near worse than this. Unless you want your apple-crumble smelling brother, Raphael, to take your place at Jack's side, I would suggest that you get your vanilla scented ass together and recover from this quickly. Use his energy to find your way back.

Alex removed his talons from Miguel's head. He hunched over the ice chest for a moment to collect himself and formalize a plan, while staring at Miguel's frozen face. "Good luck brother."

Alex rubbed his fingers together, sliding them in a circular motion, taking note of the silver dusting that coated his fingertips, thick like mercury and yet with the viscosity of Di-Methicone.

"Angel, you making dust already? You're going to be just fine." Alex smiled and wiped his hands over Miguel's body. "You're going to need all the help you can get."

"Raphael, he's all yours and if you get inspired to help him find the way, don't be shy."

"Alexander, I—"

"It's not a debate Raphael, just a suggestion. Don't think of it as defiance, just do the right thing." Alex smiled before turning his attention to Jack. "Stay by Raphael here. I'm going under and can't keep my eyes on you, okay. You'll be safer here."

He turned to Augy and Max motioning to them to follow him beyond Jack's earshot.

"Augy, I want a detail around Miguel and Jack, I don't want anything to happen to them. I'm not sure I trust our newest archangel. Keep Doc with her too. Max, I want you to find out everything you can on your mother. I think something has changed with her. But she has Sam somewhere and you probably are the only one who can find them. When you've found them, wait for me before you move and make sure Augy is with you at all times. Augy do not let him leave the tower without you and definitely keep him from Jack."

Alex looked back into the room frowning upon the chaos. "Jack," he whispered.

He watched as her head turned to stare at him. He smiled. "Be safe."

She nodded.

"Let Jesus out, please."

Alex watched Jesus slink out of the bathroom door. He smiled as he watched the hound bare all of his teeth at the archangel. Alex noted Raphael raise an eyebrow; the match would be no contest. Alex chuckled at the hound's determination, even though he wouldn't stand a chance against the archangel.

"Jesus, ven aqui," Alex whistled to get the hound's attention. "Zeus come here buddy. Let's go get Lina." The hound came bounding towards him.

Catching him, Alex tapped a rift.

CHAPTER TWENTY-ONE

Alex and Jesus landed in what looked like a city in the second level of hell. Every building looked like a nightclub. Music poured out of every orifice, luring lost souls into the web of abandon.

"C'mon Zeus," Alex walked up to the first nightclub.

"No dogs," The bouncer folded his arms.

"He's not a dog per se," Alex smiled. "Let me pass."

"No pets," The bouncer didn't move.

Alex vamped dropping the cadence of his voice to a preternatural level and freeing his black leathery wings. "The end of your second life would arrive quickly should you challenge me once more, daemon. Recognize me or not, I am the Under Lord of both the Fifth and Sixth Level and will pass with my hound as I wish."

The bouncer swallowed.

"Oh he's fine. He's with me. No need for any theatrics."

Alex spun around to find Lucifer decked out in a black tone on tone striped tuxedo; balancing his top hat on the edge of his head of slicked back hair. Alex thought Lucifer looked like an old twenties mobster.

"To what do I owe this pleasure?" Alex smiled.

"Hello to you, too, son."

"Don't play games with me, where's my wife." Alex whispered in Lucifer's ear as he greeted him in a one armed embrace for public display. Being in the first two levels of hell still meant that there were a lot of humans present.

"Always straight to the point Alexander. Never losing focus. My daughter could learn a lot from you."

"Where is she?"

"Like a pit-bull locked onto his catch. You know that could also be a flaw." Lucifer bared his canines and shook his head like a feral dog.

The environment changed. Alex found himself standing with Lucifer in the catacombs on some level of hell.

"Where are we now?"

"So many questions. Where is she? Where am I? Where are you?"

Alex growled.

"Down boy. She is getting what she deserves. I warned her."

"Where is she?"

"I condemned her beyond the Styx, to an eternity of harpies picking the new regenerated flesh from her bones."

"What happened to the children she carried."

"She was not with child when she went to the harpies."

Blood tears ran freely down Alex's face.

"Such a tender emotion, perhaps you do have a heart after all?"

Alex roared with rage shaking the catacombs.

"Pure anger, even better. I love it," Lucifer giggled.

"I want my wife."

"You'll have to go get her and if you make it there. Good luck trying to get back."

"I'll make it back with her."

"Oh and what about the Keeper? With her Angel of Light down and her Angel of Darkness gone, who will look after her?"

Alex stared at Lucifer and snapped his fangs close. He shook off his anger and furnished a smile worthy of any executive of hell. "Know this Lucifer. It is in your best interest that I remain the Vassal Warrior for Darkness. You have no other that can match, let alone outrank an archangel. While you may be able to muster a daemon, which can even stand next to the Keeper without trying to eat her, you'll never find anything as versatile as I am with the power that I have. So just know if something happens to me, you have automatically tipped the scales in favor of the light."

Alex watched as Lucifer roared, dissipating into the side of the rock walls in anger.

"Fuck. Lina how am I going to find you?" Alex sunk against the cool side of the rock and slid down into a seated position. "Zeus?" Alex could swear he heard a sniffing.

"Jesus?" Alex whistled.

His hell hound appeared growling and snarling down the hallway.

Alex jumped to his feet. "Hey boy."

The hound bounded towards him wagging his tail.

"Let's go find Lina. Donde esta Mama?" Alex ventured in his best Spanish.

Jesus put his nose to the ground and set off through the combs. Alex jogged after him through miles of combs until they came to an opening.

Jesus sniffed the cavern, first stopping at a pool of blood. The hound exhaled and moved onward. Alex bent over the aged blood which had mixed with the sandy floor. He picked some up and rubbed it thoughtfully between his fingers. Particles of silver dust infused the blood laden sand. "Miguel."

Flashes of Miguel's memories bombarded him. *He was attacked here by multiple lower daemons that crawled over him, like ants on a chocolate muffin left behind from a picnic. Lucifer shredded Miguel's wings in his weakened condition. Lina was thrown to the other side of the cavern.*

She tried to help; Lucifer sent a fireball at Miguel and ejected him to the penthouse.

A howl from Jesus brought his attention back to the cavern. "The last thing Miguel saw was Lucifer's hand on Lina's stomach."

Alex jumped up and ran over to Jesus. "What did you find boy?"

Jesus howled again and licked Alex's face, disintegrating his skin with the caustic acid from his tongue.

"There's a lot of blood here. Something went wrong." Alex brought the blood stained sand to his nose, "It's Lina. Find her Zeus."

Alex put his hand on Jesus' collar and the hound took off through the wall. Alex braced himself for impact, but the wall dematerialized as soon as the hound touched it. He bounded through walls and floors, descending through the layers of hell. After a while, Alex found it easier to keep up with Jesus by opening his wings and gliding after him.

Suddenly, Jesus came to a full stop at the river Styx.

Alex knelt by the hound's side. Jesus nudged him onward. "I'm going, old boy, but you have to go home. This is where your journey ends. Go home, we'll be there soon."

Alex wondered what the hound was thinking; his eyes were black and unblinking. Alex couldn't discern a single emotion or traipse of thought. "Go home!" Alex raised his voice.

He thought he heard a scream; he turned his head towards the mists of the Styx, peering through them.

Alex walked along the river bank until he came to a small jetty. Reaching into his pocket, he extracted a gold coin and the note he had taken from Blondie that he kept meaning to read. He flicked the coin into the swirling mists of the Styx and listened for the splash that the coin might have made if it hit the water. Instead, he saw the mist take the form of a boat traversing the water towards him. No time to read the note now, he shoved it back into the depths of his pants pocket.

The boat docked by the jetty, Alex told Jesus one last time to go home then boarded the boat ensuring that the hound couldn't follow.

CHAPTER TWENTY-TWO

Alex gave one last look towards the bank, hoping to see Jesus; the mists were too thick. They swirled around him sending shivers down his spine.

The crunch of the unmanned boat against the opposing shore broke Alex's attention. He looked around and moved cautiously down the boat and swung his legs over, thankful to feel solid ground.

Voices pierced through the mists the moment his feet connected with the ground.

"You shouldn't have come," they said.

"Lina," Alex called hopefully. Visibility was thin; he could barely see a few feet in front of him.

This is some different kind of hell. A far cry from the fire and brimstone that I have seen, this is the kind of hell that makes you crazy. Alex thought as he trudged forward. *Lina I swear if you are anywhere in here I will find you. Alex attempted to connect with her mentally.*

"Alejandro?"

"Lina, where are you my love?"

"You'll never find me, go home."

"I won't leave you here."

"You will never find me. It's futile. Just go."

"Why don't you believe me when I tell you I have come for you and I will find you?"

"That Amor is exactly why you won't. This is hell; your desires will always be beyond your reach. You will never find me, because they will keep shifting me before you reach me."

"Who are they?"

"The harpies"

He heard her sigh telepathically. "Hold on honey, hold on. I'm going to think of something. Can they hear us?"

"No, I don't think they are telepathic"

"So, you have both sisters right now watching you?"

"Both? Sisters?"

Alex detected the confusion in her voice. "Yes both of the harpies?"

"There are three of them here and I suppose they could be sisters."

"Hang tight honey."

Alex stood tall and bulked himself up for a fight. He unsnapped his dark leathery wings and stretched them to the fullest, as he tilted his head back and roared squeezing his eyes shut as he unleashed his power.

"Hear me now this Sub Level of Hell, I am Alexander. I demand an audience with Aello and Celaeno. I am the Underlord for the Fifth and Sixth Levels of Hell. How dare you not acknowledge me?"

Alex felt the environment changing, almost as if the mists stopped touching him. He opened his eyes and found that the mists were indeed retracting, cutting a clear path. He trudged forth with a dominating and authoritative air, until he came to a clearing.

As the mists parted, green grass greeted him, surrounded by tall pine trees. The height of the trees drew his eyes upward to the blue skies. Alex inhaled sharply at the onset of screaming that seemed to come from the depths of the trees.

"Lina," he whispered, snapping his wings closed and lunging towards the screams; he stopped short and eyed the two harpies that dropped out of the sky before him obscuring his path. Half bird and half woman; the front half very much a woman and the back all bird. A beak replaced the nose with iridescent feathers stemming from the beak upwards and down the back, forming glorious plumage. A drunkard might mistake the front of the harpie for a beautiful naked woman if he never looked above her mouth or below her thighs, for even her feet ended in talons rivaling those of any bird of prey.

"Who are you?" Alex demanded. "Where are Aello and Celaeno?"

"You call the names of our old ones freely."

"I would have a word with them, where are they?" Alex watched as the two harpies stared at each other. Something wasn't right in the harpie hierarchy.

"They are not here. What do you want with them?" the harpie with the green plumage peered at him.

"What I want with the elders is between me and those of command. You are clearly not in command. You have no understanding of the ways. If you cannot give me what I want, my business here is done." Alex turned to leave.

"You cannot leave," the green feathered harpie glared.

"And why is that?" Alex sneered allowing gold flame of rage to flicker in his eyes.

"Because once you cross over to this side of hell, no one can leave. You are stuck here."

Alex gritted his teeth and growled at the harpies. "I don't know why I'm wasting my time with the two of you underlings. Either take me to your current leadership, or get out of my way before I break both of your silly necks. Of course, I can leave; I am an Underlord of Hell." Alex hoped that his act was convincing.

The harpies' talons closed around each of his arms and they took off towards the sky.

As they flew, he stared downwards hoping to trace their path; the mists obscured his vision. Flashes of light lit up the cloud cover; that he presumed was hell changing the scenery for each lost soul that had crossed over.

CHAPTER TWENTY-THREE

Jack peered into the ice box and stared at Miguel's unchanging face. *He truly does have a frosty look.*

Her mind wandered, listening to Max and Augy talk about the company's infiltration. The unfamiliar deep rumble of Dr. Ferguson's voice chiming in now and again, made her wonder how many other supernatural entities existed.

Jack turned her head back to Miguel and the no less beautiful Raphael standing over him. His copper skin glowed and his amber, brown, gold plumage was brilliant; nothing compared to the stony brilliance of Miguel's platinum plumage with hints of blue.

What happened Mig? Jack leaned over the icebox. *I don't understand what you could have possibly done. Why won't they help you? Why did you lose your wings?* Jack grabbed his frozen hand.

"You should be careful; he is in a dangerous state right now. He could hurt you."

Jack looked at Raphael and moved his cautionary hand away. "He would never hurt me. I'll be okay," she turned her attention back to Miguel. *You're not on your own. I'm right here and I'm not going anywhere until this is all figured out.*

Jack stared at the angel, hoping for a sign that he heard her. She jumped when she saw his eyes fly open. His hands reached for her, pulling her into him. His mouth opened, revealing two elongated canines. Jack felt them pierce her neck just as the weight of the lid to the ice box descended upon her. Darkness shrouded her vision.

"Jack!"

She heard her name being called urgently. She opened her eyes, surprised to see Miguel standing before her. "Where are we?" Miguel appeared to be standing on clouds and she, sitting on them. "Did I die? Are we in heaven?"

"No," Miguel smiled, "we are in my stasis."

Jack felt her neck. "Did you bite me, or was that just a dream?"

"I bit you."

Jack jumped to her feet landing in Miguel's arms; unsteady on the cloudy platform. Standing in clouds felt like walking on an air mattress.

"Easy there," he smiled, displaying his usual perfect smile.

Jack pushed him off, looking for the missing canines. "I didn't know you had teeth like that?" she resisted the urge to peel back his lips and inspect his mouth. The smile that she had grown accustomed to never revealed canines.

"Everything revolves around blood. Angels don't have to take blood like vampires, because our systems are evolved and more aged than the vampire, but we aren't very different, I suppose. Although not many would actually compare themselves."

"Why did you bite me? You didn't even ask," Jack folded her arms with annoyance.

"There was no time. I needed to explain. It was the only way to bring you here."

Jack softened. "Am I okay, can I go back?"

"At any time you want to return, I'll send you back. The latch to unlock the lid to the icebox is on the inside. You'll have to turn over to reach it. But I'm sure that there are plenty of people trying to get you out right about now."

"Okay then, what was so important?"

"I think they made a deal," Miguel pointed upwards and downwards.

Jack nodded signifying her understanding and asked, "Why would they do that? I thought they were enemies?"

"No, that is a common misconception, they are adversaries. However, even adversaries may strike a deal in the event that an outcome advantageous to them may be affected. In this case, I believe that they feared the three babies that Lina carried."

"Why? What's so special about them?"

"I don't know, except that I observed that they each created circumstances that made it difficult for Lina. Each time she lost a child, they triumphed. I had to be sure that the last child lived. There was a bad seed, a good seed, and an unknown. It is the latter that lived. Corruptible either way, I think this is the one they feared."

"Wow! I would never have imagined. I thought that you and Lina were you know... I mean I wasn't the only one. Alex thought so, too. I didn't know what to say. You know?" Jack shrugged her shoulders.

"No, I don't know," Miguel looked confused.

"Okay, I thought the two of you were hooking up," Jack stared at Miguel intently. His face seemed to be constrained somehow. "Well?"

Jack sighed as he burst out laughing.

"Even in my weakened condition, that laugh felt good." Miguel was still chuckling between his words. "I was helping her because she felt estranged from Alexander. I thought that you and I shared something special, to be honest with you; I know now that you also are in love with Alexander."

Jack sighed again. "That is such a complicated subject Mig. I do love him, but I don't know why I can't seem to just give myself to him. He can't say he loves me. Do I want him to at this point? I don't know. I just don't know." Jack sunk into the clouds and placed her head on Miguel's shoulder when he sat next to her.

"And me?" Miguel asked.

Jack felt his arm wrap around her. "Every time, I think that we have something, you disappear and I'm never really sure. It's like we never have a chance to grow anything." Jack twisted her head to look into his eyes. "Mig, I know this. My heart hurt to see you in such pain. I knew that no matter how many other people did not want to stand by your side, I would, until the truth told me that you had betrayed me and our goals. I know we have more than just a friendship; how much more I don't know."

"It's a start," Miguel smiled.

Jack felt him lean forward and kiss her. Warmth evaded her, a tightness formed in the pit of her belly, mingling with a growing hunger. As the kiss ended, Jack opened her eyes full of questions only to find herself face-to-face with the frozen Miguel.

Wow, that was awesome. I never imagined anything so intense and easy to believe in; maybe I should have.

Jack twisted around, her lips chattering, to search for the latch. She exhaled painfully in relief having found it. Pulling on it, the lid opened.

She screamed seeing an axe poised above her head. "What? Are you guys' crazy? What the fuck are you going to do, cut my head off?" Jack jumped out of the ice box closing the lid hastily.

"Put the axe down Augy," Jack pointed at the confused vampire.

"We thought you were a gonner," Augy raised an eyebrow, "seems like we were all confused."

"What is that?" Max asked.

"What are you talking about?"

"You've been kissed by an angel, while we've been out here worrying for your safety," Raphael chuckled.

Jack walked over to a mirror. *Holy crapola would you look at that?* The reflection showed her lips coated in a pale blue metallic lipstick, except Jack knew she hadn't applied any lipstick. Taking her fingers to her lips, she rubbed the substance between her fingers. Pausing for a moment, she couldn't decide if it were a platinum blue or a pale blue; either way, it wasn't coming off in a hurry.

A cough behind her brought her attention back to her audience.

"So, what did he tell you?"

Jack wondered if Raphael's smile was genuine. Undecided how the information should be used, she decided to wait for Alex's return. "Oh, I don't know that anyone here would be interested." she touched her lips and pouted as she had seen Lina do, for good measure. Satisfied that they turned their attention away from her and Miguel, she sunk into a nearby chair to figure out how to get a hold of Alex.

CHAPTER TWENTY-FOUR

The cavern was dank. Screams echoed around the walls reverberating pain and suffering. Alex recognized the cadence of Lina's voice through the screams. He allowed the rage to build within him, hoping that none would see the sadness he felt at his wife's suffering.

"How much further? My patience is trying," Alex growled.

The green feathered harpie responded by stepping to the side and opening her arm, encouraging him to step into the opening. *A water source must have hollowed out the maze of interconnecting caverns*, Alex mused as he stepped into the opening.

The sights that greeted him both angered and sickened him. Lina lay spread eagled pinned to the mountainside. She was bound with magical restraints that prohibited her shifting. He observed harpies picking the flesh off her bones. She was being allowed to regenerate just enough for another harpie to attack. Other harpies lay dead on the floor, presumably from her ability to use magic and launch fireballs. In her weakened condition; they weren't effective.

You came.

Lina's mental connection was weak.

Of course.

I thought your voice was a dream.

Alex stifled a smile. I would never leave you anywhere.

What about Jack?

What about her? She's fine.

I thought that you wouldn't leave her.

I don't want to talk about her or Miguel right now. I want you back safely then we'll talk and figure things out. I can't bear to see you like this.

The babies…

Soon enough babes, I promise you, we will have our turn. First things first, let's get out of here.

Alex tore his eyes away from Lina. Looking around the caven, he saw Aello and Celeano locked behind bars in their own den, covering their bodies with their wings. He was surprised to see hope flit across their eyes; they recognized him. It had been at least a good century since their last encounter.

Alex eyed the harpie sitting on the throne surrounded by lesser harpies in poor condition. Feathers were strewn across the floor; the creatures themselves were in better condition. Many lay sick or dying across the cavern. Alex realized that he had arrived in the midst of a power struggle.

He stepped over a body with feigned disgust, as he caught a glimpse of the light disappearing from the creature's eyes before it died.

"What in the name of Abaddon is going on here?"

"You have come at an inconvenient time, Underlord," the harpie on the throne screeched.

"I demand to know who addresses me, and why I am being greeted in such filthy conditions," Alex sneered baring a fang.

"I am Eataline."

"Your lineage?" Alex queried, "do you no longer declare your lineage?"

"How do you know our customs, Underlord and of what importance is it to you?" Eataline screeched again.

"I need to be sure that I am speaking to the rightful commander. How do I know that you are where you should be? The message I have is for a particular set of ears. If yours are not those, I will have to kill you." Alex used his speed to reappear on the other side of the throne. He placed his hands around the harpie's neck, allowing his talons to extend and pierce her flesh. "Am I understood?"

"The seat is mine. What gives you reason to believe it is not?" Eataline gasped, her hands clutching at Alex's iron grip.

"You don't have the memories to rule Underling," Alex released his grip and walked around the throne. He kept his voice at a whisper. "I will make a deal with you."

"What do you want?" Eataline rubbed her throat.

"I want the fallen Prince."

"What deal could you possibly make for her?" Eataline leaned forward staring at Alex.

Alex noted her beak dangerously close to his face. He could see the down forming new feathers at the edge of her beak. Orange and red feathers, contrasting with greens and yellows glistened over her face. She was a beauty as harpies went. Alex was sure she had a warrior's strength to match if she had made it to the throne.

Still, he didn't flinch as he closed the gap; daringly moving his face to her right to get closer to her ear, he whispered, "Every day you guard your throne because you have to defend what's yours by force. You are not recognized as having the rightful ownership to the throne. You do not have the memories to understand how to help your subjects recognize you. Your elders do not recognize you. What if you could have these memories? What if you didn't have to fight everyday of your life? What if you could rule as they ruled?"

Alex felt Eataline take a sharp intake of breath.

"You could make this happen?"

"I could help you," Alex cast a glance at Aello and Celano, who were straining their ears to hear the conversation. "I would tell you how to gain an audience with the Keeper and I could talk to her about you."

"What would that give me?" Eataline gripped the throne.

"Should she determine that you are the rightful owner to the throne based on everything you have waged, the memories will transfer from the elders to you by right."

"And all you want is the Prince?" Eataline sat deeper in the throne.

Alex nodded.

"You would have me defy the King himself?"

"Was the request made of you?"

"Not of me, but a predecessor."

"Then you owe nothing, as you have made no pact."

Alex eyed Eataline, as she applied some thought. He stuck out his taloned hand. "Do we have a deal?"

He was surprised by how firm she responded with her grip.

"We have a deal Underlord."

As soon as Alex's hand was freed, he leapt to Lina's side. Using his vampiric speed, he removed her ties and took a rift to a remote part in the forest in harpie world.

"Lina."

Alex stared at his wife; her pale and tattered skin barely covered her skeleton. He laid her gently on the silted floor of the cave. The ebb of blood flowing to regenerate her slowed. Alex glanced around the cave, he reached out to grab some smaller branches off nearby trees to blockade the entrance.

Lina, he attempted a mental connection. No response. Taking a talon, he sliced his neck, nicking his carotid. He positioned himself to allow the blood to spill onto her lips. "C'mon baby." Alex raised her head helping the blood to reach her system.

With preternatural quickness, Lina's body rose unnaturally latching onto his neck with all four canines. Her talons gripped onto him with predatory strength, her survival instinct dominating her being.

Alex roared in pain, but he bit into her to balance the blood between both bodies, and guide her back from a feral state.

Why did you come Alex?

I love you Lina, I couldn't let you go like this.

You should have let me die.

Never.

What about Jack?

What about her? I thought you were okay with her?

I understand that you love her; it felt more so her than me?

I do feel for her. You are right. But Jack and I can never be. We can never have what you and I have. I have a role to play in her life which has created a line that I can never cross. Besides, why would I risk a life with you, an eternity together over a momentary hundred years or so? If you didn't come along, then yes, I may have pursued Jack and sometimes I admit I may fall into old habits with her, but I try Lina I do. You came along and you changed everything, everything. I don't want to lose that.

Alex felt her fangs retract. He pulled away and stared into the glistening brown eyes of his once again beautiful and vibrant wife. Her lustrous black curls framed her olive skin. Alex continued, "As we are baring souls, I will also admit I felt a bit of jealousy towards Miguel."

Lina squinted her eyes, "Miguelito?"

"Yes, our vanilla scented Angel Miguel."

"Why him?"

"You two were spending an awful lot of time together. Everywhere I turned, your scents were intermingled. I couldn't stand it, or help but think…"

"No way Amor," Lina purred as she placed her finger on his lips.

"Seriously Lina, you even have a pet name for him. Who wouldn't have thought?"

"Amor know this…"

Alex closed his eyes holding her in his arms, feeling her draw blood in little daemon bites from his neck. He felt his shirt rip, as she continued down his torso. Alex ran his hands through her hair feeling her undo the buckle of his pants. "Woman are you well enough?"

He roared in a mixture of pain and ecstasy as she bit into his penis, he became fully erect. Pulling her up towards him, he felt her full breasts hovering above his mouth. Suckling them, he felt Lina's back arch while he teased her right nipple.

The sensation of overwhelming warmth enveloped his engorged penis, as Lina straddled him. He ran his hands down her smooth back, cupping her taut buttocks, as she moved her hips to a rhythm he realized he had missed.

Alex's breath came ragged as Lina bit into him, claiming him as hers, until they collapsed post climax.

He lay with his head on her chest staring down at her flat belly. A faint scar traced a jagged line across her abdomen, meeting up with her linea negra – a small reminder that something had been stolen from them.

"Papi… I…" Lina started.

"Come, woman," Alex's voice was gruff with emotion. "We have some work to do. We will have plenty of time to rest later. Can you travel?"

Lina nodded.

Alex gathered his clothes giving Lina his ripped shirt, he donned his pants. "Now, how do we get out of here?"

Lina smiled. Putting her fingers to her lips, she whistled. "Jesus, come get us!"

"Jesus?" Alex queried with amusement creeping into his eyes.

"Yes," Lina laughed, "he is hell's best kept secret."

"How many more like him are there?"

"None," Lina frowned. "Daddy killed them all off"

"All?"

"There was once a creature named Kerberos."

"I remember those stories."

"He had fifty heads and was the guardian to the gates of hell. It was Kerberos that would stop those who crossed over from escaping. Kerberos could traverse all levels of hell into terra to retrieve the souls that hell claimed."

"I didn't see such a creature and I've been all over hell and across the Styx and back." Alex mused.

"That's because Daddy thought the creature had too much freedom, especially after one day it responded favorably to a soul that paid it some kindness."

"What happened?"

"Daddy killed it and cut off all of the heads, save one."

"So how did Jesus come about?"

"I saved the last Kerberos head that was attached to the body and revived it. I renamed him Jesus. I didn't want Daddy to find out."

"Always defying Daddy dearest, "Alex laughed, as the hound came bounding through the brush. "Wow, who would have imagined. Zeus. Good to see you old boy," Alex bent over to scratch the hound behind his ears. "Home?" he raised a quizzical eyebrow at his smiling wife.

"I have to get something from my chambers on the 6th level first, presuming that Daddy dearest has left it untouched. I'll meet you home."

"Not likely sweetness, I'm not leaving your side if I can help it until I know this is all over." Alex grinned as he gripped Jesus' collar.

CHAPTER TWENTY-FIVE

The fires blazed as Lina walked into her chambers with Alex and Jesus in tow. The flames cast millions of shadowy faces over the rock walls with gaping mouths emitting silent screams.

Lina stood before her closet doors. She snapped her fingers and smiled as the doors opened. She allowed Alex's shirt to slip off and smiled when she caught his lustful stares. Happy that she was not the only one reveling in her beauty, Lina turned her attention back to her closet and selected a pale red ochre dragon skin dress. The red dragon was the strongest of all creatures; his skin would give her strength and protection.

She slipped into the dress feeling strength and confidence flowed into her system.

"Wow! You look amazing."

Lina smiled. She smoothed her hands down the dress, feeling safe, having covered herself in the strongest armor in all realms - dragon skin. Her smile faded as they reached her hips, "It's funny how a good dress can make you feel incredible even though on the inside…" Lina cast a glance at Alex, so much remained unspoken between them. She wondered if they would ever have a chance to talk about things.

"We will make things right," Alex sighed. Getting up off the bed, he crossed the room to embrace her.

"My father is coming, we must hurry." Still holding onto Alex, Lina grabbed a small drawstring bag from her dresser.

"What's in there?" Alex queried.

"I want to make a viewing pool so I can search the realms of hell from above." Turning to Jesus, she said, "Stay, and guard my room, okay?"

The hound sneezed and lay down making a noise that closely resembled grumbling.

"C'mon Amor we have to go," Lina held onto Alex and tapped a rift.

The colors in the fabric of time were bright like the spectrum created from the sun's rays hitting a prism. Lina rested her head comfortably against Alex's chest. His voice ran through her head like a stuck record. "We will make things right."

But how? What could ever make things right again?

"Something is very wrong," Lina heard Alex's voice rumble. Raising her head, she noticed the dark blue aura swirling around their heads.

"We are no longer in time's rift," Lina looked around her muttering in Spanish. "This is a daemon summoning. Except, normally the spell doesn't wait for me, it throws me up there. Perhaps because we were intertwined it cannot bring you, too." Lina looked into Alex's eyes. "I cannot leave you here, because you will fade with the spell."

"Then I will go through with you and fly straight upwards, perhaps the one who summons will not notice."

"I don't know about that, unless it's an inexperienced witch; then again, it takes a seasoned witch, or warlock to call a daemon of my level." Lina was thoughtful for a moment. "Okay, we don't have much of a choice. We'll try it. Maybe we'll get lucky."

Lina threw him upwards, while climbing up him with catlike daemonic speed. Once through the portal, she jettisoned Alex upward, while shrouding their entrance in mist giving him a chance to crawl along the ceiling into the next room.

"Who dares summon me?" Lina made her voice echo off every particle in the mist.

"It is I, Lady Stanfield of the New Jersey coven that calls you daemon"

Lina levitated, turning to face Mrs. Stanfield. She regarded the old woman, wondering what she wanted. Mrs. Stanfield was Max's biological mother in name only; she had given away her son a long time ago to Alex. "What do you want good witch," Lina spat the last word in disgust, clearing the mist to get a better look at her.

"Who came through with you daemon? I sense another," Mrs. Stanfield demanded.

"Know whom you have called?" Lina purred. "Address me by my rightful title. Is that what you really want to know? Who accompanied me through the portal? Information comes with a price. Ask wisely."

Mrs. Stanfield smiled. "I have a sacrifice for you."

"And what would a good witch be calling a daemon of my stature with the offering of a sacrifice for?"

"I am a witch by rite. Should that not be enough?"

"Well, you were able to muster the summoning. Speak on."

"I have a young witch that may be of special interest to you."

"How so? Bring her to me and I will gauge her worth," Lina saw Alex watching and cautioned him not to interfere lest the spell go awry. "Hmm, a witch for a question."

"Crowned Prince of all Abbadon, I do not wish for a question. I have a request."

"Make it with care witch," Lina furrowed her eyebrows deepening her voice.

"I want you to kill my son, Maxwell Stanfield."

"How curious that a mother wishes to kill her own child,"

The woman looked her dead in the eyes in disgust.

"He has been dead to me for many years and now he has become mixed up in all kinds of evil doings."

"Such a request requires a sacrifice."

"She is a Tru-blood witch."

"Bring me this witch. I will assess her worthiness as a sacrifice based on your request."

Lina watched as Mrs. Stanfield left the room, her drab dark potato sack of clothing making swishing noises as she walked.

Alex

Yes my love, came the response.

For this spell to close, I have to take a witch. You must make it so that it is the Stanfield witch and not whomever she is bringing.

I think she is bringing Sam.

Why does she have Sam?

I don't know, but we've been looking for her and all last reports are that Stanfield took her.

Well, if I touch Sam, she'll become the sacrifice. So it's either Stanfield or Sam.

Then it'll have to be Stanfield.

What will we tell Max?

The truth, his mother tried to kill both him and Sam; we had to make a decision.

Fair enough. Lina wondered how Max would respond.

I think he'll be happy to have Sam back. He's been worried sick about her.

Amor, here she comes and she has Sam.

Lina extended the column to hide Alex. She wondered if Sam could see Alex. She turned to look directly at him as she passed by. Alex placed his forefinger vertically across his lips in the universal signal for silence.

Lina began to laugh as Mrs. Stanfield returned presenting Sam to her.

"This witch has already been sacrificed."

"Then how does she live?" Mrs. Stanfield queried.

"How I use my sacrifices is none of your business," Lina made flames burst around her, emulating her feigned rage.

"Do you accept the sacrifice?"

Lina squinted her eyes staring at Sam. "I'm not sure this little witch meets the value required to kill your son."

Lina watched the impact of her words reanimate Sam; she wondered just how weak she was. Sam began screaming and chanting. Lina watched as she activated her wards and threw up shields.

"See, she is worth it. I just want to know that Maxwell Stanfield is dead."

"Done!" Lina snapped. "I will take a witch for that task."

Mrs. Stanfield's eyes opened wide. The impact from Alex's feet pushed her toward Lina's open arms.

Lina watched smiling, as the older witch flew to her. She saw Alex grab onto Sam through the wards; Lina sent them both flying for good measure, not wanting either of them to be sucked into the spell's portal once it closed.

She bared her fangs with the Stanfield witch safely in her arms. "Your son Maxwell Stanfield is dead to you and has been so for quite a while."

"I saw him a few days ago, he lives."

"He walks terra no more as a Stanfield, he is truly Macedo offspring now."

"Will you kill him?"

"Your last request witch was only for knowledge. This you now have. Your request has been fulfilled." Lina sank her fangs into her carotid, draining her memories. Blood tears fell as she witnessed the birth of Max and wondered about her own child."

Lina took a deep breath, as she condemned the sacrificial body to the Styx. She wiped the blood from her face before materializing in the Stanfield New Jersey house, where Alex and Sam were waiting.

Sam was bent over the lifeless body of Alex muttering, "I'm so sorry, I didn't know."

"What's going on?" Lina walked up to them.

"I'm so sorry Lina, I didn't know it was Alex. I didn't mean to hurt him. Is he…?"

"What happened?"

"I had my wards and shields up, Alex grabbed me and he's been burned, maybe even killed." Sam's eyes brimmed with tears. "I don't know why the shields didn't recognize him."

"We've just come from below, so we are coated in a layer of evil. They recognized him because he's only burned. If they didn't, he would be chopped into little pieces and a little harder to regenerate."

Alex groaned.

"See," Lina smiled, "he'll be just fine. You're getting very powerful Sam. You might consider some training to help you maintain some control over it as it grows."

Sam nodded.

"I do have to give him blood to help him regenerate, so we can all travel to the Macedo Tower."

Sam nodded. "I'll go get a few things." "C'mon Amor. At this rate, we'll have to start a score board of how many times who saves who, before we get home." Lina winced as she shoved her lanced hand into Alex's mouth. Feeling his teeth sink into her wrist, she maneuvered herself around him so her legs straddled his torso; his back rested on her abdomen. Leaning forward, she sank her fangs into his neck to balance the blood draw, satisfied that his primal instinct for survival had kicked in.

When Alex had regenerated fully, they released their hold on each other.

"What happened?" he asked leaning his head on her breasts.

"Sam's wards and shields got you."

"She's getting strong."

"I recommended training for her."

Alex nodded.

Lina heard Sam's footsteps. "She's coming." She wiped her mouth and kissed the blood off of Alex's.

CHAPTER TWENTY-SIX

"Aww, you guys are so cute together."

Alex smiled, as he rose to his feet to help Lina up. "Sam," he held his arms out. "It's so good to see you. Max is worried about you. Well, we all were, and I'm so glad to have great news to take back to him."

"Take back to him?"

Alex watched the cloud build in Sam's face. "I'm not sure he's ready yet, Sam. I'm just worried for the both of you. He's still working on his control."

"I haven't seen him since you took him. It feels like an eternity. Besides," Sam smiled, "I've been working on something for him."

Alex took a little plastic piece from Sam's upheld palm and examined it. "What is this? It looks like a mouth retainer."

"Well it is, sort of. But it is spelled. It should stop his fangs from biting while he wears it, plus it should stave off the hunger for a while. Kinda how Nicorette works for smokers."

Alex face became serious as he gave back the mouthpiece to Sam. "Except you know that this is not a habit he can kick, and if you use your wards on him you could kill him."

"I know, I just want to be with him, and hoped that this would give him time to deter him from biting me."

"I don't know, Sam." Alex shook his head.

"We have to figure it out. He can kill me if he bites me and I him if I shield. We have to figure it out. Please let me have this chance?" Sam clasped her hands over Alex's.

"I think it's a good idea," Lina piped in.

"It doesn't hurt to try," Alex's voice faded.

"What is it?" Lina asked.

"It's Jack. We have to go." Alex beckoned everyone together.

"All of us? Why don't we meet you at the Tower?" Lina offered.

"We stick together. We are stronger that way." Alex grabbed everyone and tapped the rift following Jack's call.

Once he landed, he set Lina and Sam on the floor. Jumping over them, he freed his wings and dropped his fang. To his surprise, Jack was standing in front him; hands akimbo, looking intimidating.

"What's wrong?" Alex asked retracting his fangs.

"You used me." Jack stabbed him in the chest with her finger.

"Hello to you, too, I ask again, what is wrong?" Alex rubbed his chest at the point the offending finger attempted entry.

"You used my position to your benefit."

Alex looked at the rage flying across Jack's face. "What on earth are you talking about?"

Jack pointed her finger towards the closed doors of the magistrate courtroom in Peace Palace. "I have three harpies in there fighting over a throne and all of them said that you made promises that I would…"

Alex held up a finger silencing Jack. "I understand how this must look; it was a precarious situation. I never promised anything. I did make mention that I would talk to you about them and their goings on. If they inferred that I meant to influence you; that could have been a mistake on their part, as I never made such promises."

Jack folded her hands. "Hmpf."

"I have a witness."

"Who?"

"Me?" Lina stepped forward ducking under Alex's wings.

"Lina, I'm so glad you are okay," Jack rushed forward giving her a hug. "Sam? Oh my goodness. Alex, you just have a bunch of good news with you," Jack mumbled embracing Sam.

"Okay, okay," Jack brushed invisible dirt from her clothes.

Alex watched as she steeled herself again.

"What about these harpies?"

"Just listen to their story. Ask about their culture. You must figure out who is the rightful owner to the throne based on their laws.

"How do I know what their laws are?"

"Ask for them."

"Can't you just tell me?"

Alex glared at Jack. "I could, but that may be considered influencing you. I only committed to talking to you about them."

"So?"

"Aello and Celano are the elders and original harpie leadership. I do not know by who, or how they were up-seated. I do know that this red and green harpie called Eataline, has the strength, but not the memories to lead, which makes it dangerous. Where is Raphael?"

"He is in there?" Jack nodded towards the courtroom. Alex could see she was deep in thought.

"Where is Miguel?" Lina asked.

"He is in stasis, he didn't fare so well being down there." Alex answered.

"He's going to be okay," Jack gushed. "I talked to him. I'm so sorry about everything you went through."

Alex watched Lina's face, which immediately steeled. He reached for her hand ignoring Sam's gasp.

"I have some information for you from Miguel and I think he knows more; he's waiting for you to return."

"You spoke with him while he is in stasis?"

"I did, I'll fill you in later. Let's get this over and done with and then we'll go home and plan."

Alex marched into the courtroom behind Jack, and ceremoniously took his position on her left in parallel with the unusually broody Raphael. He watched as Lina and Sam took a seat in two of the thousands of empty seats the courtroom hosted.

The conversation droned onwards until a loud screech brought Alex back to consciousness.

Eataline was threatening Jack. "You are supposed to transfer the memories to me."

"You have not persuaded me that you are the rightful heir based on Harpie Law." Jack replied looking through ancient scrolls provided by the harpie elders.

"That seat has been promised to me by many." Eataline screeched.

"None of whom are in this room," Jack answered. "And that is the problem."

"I'll kill you!" Eataline flapped her wings to rise from her position.

Alex unfolded his arms as Raphael moved from his position. A bright light blazed, as he withdrew his sword and chopped off the harpie's head. The screeching stopped.

Alex watched as Raphael wiped the blade of his sword on the dead harpie's feathers before re-sheathing it.

His gaze turned to Jack, who held her throat. Taking a deep breath, she rolled up the scrolls and turned to the original elders. "We will make copies of these ancient scrolls and return them to you. It is better that we know how to maintain the balance of your world by documents that cannot be tampered with. Any changes that are implemented must also be provided to us. The ownership is restored to you both - Aello and Celano." Jack waved her hand looking up from the scroll to see the elder harpies regain their youth and strength.

Alex chuckled. "So, Raphael, you still have some moves for a healer. You look so moody, it's comforting. You remind me of Miguel. Perhaps the stony face comes with the warrior position?"

Raphael chuckled. "Michael has always been a moody warrior. The most serious of us all. Thank you Nightwalker, I needed that laugh."

"Glad to help, because you'll not be among us long healer. Our Warrior of Light will return to us soon. We need him." Alex's grin was gone as he stepped down from the elevation. "Let's go to Miguel to see if he completed his recovery."

Raphael scowled.

Alex grinned in return. "I trust you to transport the Keeper back to my quarters at the Tower."

CHAPTER TWENTY-SEVEN

"Sam?"

"Max, you're alright," Sam scanned every pore on Max's face. His dirty blonde hair was still tousled. He was missing his glasses and his eyes seemed a little glassy; an inconsequential change at most. His smile was still beguiling and charming, though. Sam rushed into in arms, pressing herself against him. His heartbeat was gone. She hugged him tighter.

"What's wrong?" Sam asked as Max extracted himself from her arms.

He was covering his face. "Sam, I can't. Augy help me."

She watched as Augy restrained Max. Alex came to her side. "Perhaps too much emotion for him right now Sam," Alex offered.

"Oh, Maxwell you pay attention to me," Sam's voice was stern.

Max swung his head to face her. His eyes were bloodshot and his fangs extended. Foreign blue veins ran through his usually glowing skin, giving it a grayish appearance.

Sam swallowed hard. "If this is going to work, we have to work hard at this and use everything in our powers to help," She reached into her pocket and pulled out the mouthpiece. "I don't know how you feel about this, but please try this on for size. If you don't like it, we'll figure out something else."

She reached forward and placed the mouthpiece on his teeth. His head dropped forward and his body sagged in Augy's arms. "Please tell me it worked." Sam kissed his forehead, thankful not to feel the protruding veins under her lips. "Please tell me you're okay Max?"

"I am ashamed that I almost hurt you," Max lisped.

"I knew that it was a risk. I was warned that you might not be ready. I just couldn't wait. That's why I came prepared. I'm so sorry if I rushed you. I don't want things to

211

feel awkward." She rested her head against his. A sinking feeling settled on her chest.

"No, no. This is a perfect solution for right now. I couldn't ask for anything more," Max nudged her head upwards with his own. "I don't even mind that I can't talk right. All I want is to be with you."

Sam looked into Max's smiling eyes, relishing in the kiss that descended upon her. She felt the warmth flood her system as his arms embraced her.

****

Alex coughed. "I don't mean to break up the reunion; we still have a few loose ends to tie up."

Sam and Max were full of smiles as they nodded in agreement.

"I hope you understand that I can't let the two of you be alone yet. Not until we are sure." Alex looked at Augy. "Max, either Augy or I should be around you when you are with Sam; just for a while."

"Got it, Dad," Max squeezed Sam.

Alex strode over to his icebox, peering in to check on Miguel. He was pleased to see that color was restored to his face and the frost barely clung to the sides of the deep chest freezer.

Alex opened the lid to the freezer against the prolific warnings of Raphael.

"Bring him back Raphael."

"I cannot go against his decision," Raphael's face was set like stone.

"You will never be the warrior that Miguel is for that reason alone; at least he thinks, you simply follow."

Alex turned to Jack. "Honey, you have to try to bring him home."

CHAPTER TWENTY-EIGHT

Jack rubbed her hands apprehensively, aware that all eyes were upon her. "Okay. I'll do it."

"I can't allow it," Raphael stepped forward blocking her path.

"What's your reasoning?" Jack narrowed her eyes.

"You will be putting yourself personally at risk."

"This job is not an easy one. Every time we go out there, we each put our necks on the line for each other. Miguel has protected me multiple times. I have no qualms about helping him."

"I don't know if either I or, the Nightwalker will be able to help you if something happens," Raphael grumbled.

"Miguel will keep me safe," Jack quipped.

"Who will keep you safe from him?" Raphael argued.

"It's been decided. I'm going in. Stand aside." Jack glared at him. "Don't make me order you."

She peered into the ice box, relieved to see that Miguel looked like he was sleeping. All the frost had melted and the freezer was barely cold.

She climbed into the freezer with the fallen angel and kissed his lips. The icebox began to spin. Hands roved over her buttocks and up her back finding the nape of her neck. Kisses rained over her.

"Miguel."

"You came back."

"I couldn't leave you," she muttered surprised.

"I want you."

Jack arched her back. "Everyone is waiting outside."

"I don't want to hide us," Miguel whispered.

Jack felt his breath waft over her like a cool breeze. "I don't either. I just don't want an audience."

Jack found herself resting on the fluffiest of clouds. "You didn't bite me this time." She looked at him. His spiky platinum hair made so much brighter by his tanned skin and sparkling blue eyes.

"I have recovered for the most part," Miguel grinned. "May I?"

Jack cradled her head in his outstretched hand. "If Raphael guided you home, would you be having sex with him?"

Miguel laughed. "No, and we don't have to have sex either, just the touch of your hand would have woken me. But your kiss woke a fire deep within."

Jack tilted her head, warmth flooded over her. Not the intense blazing heat of lust she felt with Alex; rather slow-cooking warmth; like the nourishing warmth of soup on a cold day. The kind that made you hunger for it, as the scent hit your nose, enjoying it as you savored it and basked in the sated feeling once satisfied. Alex felt more like a shot of whisky; hot, heady, and too debilitating to really be of comfort.

Thoughts of Alex dissipated. Miguel's hands unbuttoned her shirt deftly. He unsnapped the clasp of her bra with one hand, while the other guided her breast to his mouth, allowing his tongue to find her nipples. A moan escape from her lips as Miguel's mouth teased her, uncovering a pent up want. His hands were warm; as they touched her skin, sensations flooded her being. The warmth coursing throughout her developed into a sense of urgency and to her satisfaction Miguel's fingers made short work of un-cinching her belt and removing her pants.

Jack ran her fingers up the length of his back, feeling the rise and fall of his muscles until she came to the tender nubs where his wings would have sprouted. She had no time to wonder about whether or not they would grow back, or why the nubs were even still visible. Miguel plunged into the depths of her. Jack drew a sharp breath and wrapped her legs around his waist, as her focus returned to the pleasures enveloping her.

Miguel's mouth claimed hers. Jack reached her arms around his head, as he rained kisses down her neck. Her mind stilled from questions. She moved her hips to meet his every thrust, arching her back, offering her breasts to him. Jack craved his mouth, his touch, his thrust. Sweat coated their bodies as they moved in synch. Rolling over in the clouds Jack eased herself along the length of his shaft, enjoying the feeling of fullness. She looked down at Miguel's smiling face, the hunger instantly building within her again until she Released.

"Will it be like this every time?" she asked, while lazily resting her head on Miguel's chest, post climax.

"Like what?"

"Fluffy clouds," Jack reached out. They floated through her fingers; she wondered how they could lie on them.

"Is that what you would like?"

She looked up at his questioning face. "I would like it to play out however it plays out. I don't have any designs on how it should be."

She touched her lips, delighting in the passion behind the kisses. Her thoughts turned to her fingers, as she recalled the viscous dust that had coated her lips. Sure enough, there it was on her fingers. "What is this?"

Jack watched as he took her fingers in his hands and licked them.

"Ah, that is angel dust," Miguel smiled.

"Is it edible?" she yanked her hands back staring closely at the dusted covering.

"Many humans fight for what little angel dust they encounter. They find ways to chemically reproduce it. Real angel dust produces delightful side effects of happiness for humans when consumed. Some find that elated, satisfied feeling to be very addicting. The chemically reproduced alternative has other, not so pleasant side effects. Does it bother you?"

"Am I covered in it?"

"Probably."

"Well now there's just another reason for someone to want to attack me."

"I will protect you, but I'm sensing something else?"

Jack looked up to see concern written across his face. "It's just that sometimes I feel like a walking billboard.. I have Alex's crest on the nape of my neck, Raphael's crosses on my palms, and my wards that wander about wherever they want while the aegis sits on my shoulder. The dust doesn't bother me so much; honestly it's just crazy. Sometimes I'm not sure that I'm explaining it right." Jack managed a smile.

"I don't want to remove the wards because they protect you; when the angel dust washes off, those other markings will be gone. The power behind them will still remain, but you won't be able to see them."

"Really?"

"Really," Miguel smiled.

Jack tilted her head and placed a long kiss softly on his lips. "Thank you."

"We should probably get back."

Jack nodded. "You're right."

****

The lid of the icebox creaked when it opened. All eyes turned towards it expectantly. Lina, Max, and Sam were standing around the viewing pool that Lina setup, and were searching the realms of hell using magic for traces of a newborn child.

Max was plugged into a blood supply, a straw hung from his mouth to maintain his energy. He also found a way to use his inherited magic.

Alex cast a glance at his family. His beautiful wife, son and budding warlock, and daughter-in-law to be, he was sure.

Raphael brooded against the window, not liking the role that he was being forced to play.

Augy and Doc remained by Alex's side. They had been talking about the breach until the icebox lid broke their conversation.

Miguel was the first out of the icebox -naked as he was went in; with the exception of a slight erect penis.

Alex noted that Raphael's face soured. He strode towards Miguel, placing himself between the icebox and Raphael. Miguel reached in to help Jack out.

"Hey I never thought I'd be saying this, but I'm so glad to see you," Alex laughed giving Miguel a full embrace. "What happened, they don't have clothes in stasis?"

"It was a rough recovery until the end," Miguel smiled.

"I'll bet," Alex laughed. "Dude, go find yourself some clothes in my closet. Just don't get dust on everything. As a matter of fact, why don't you guys go shower first." Alex cast a glance at Jack, who tried to shield her embarrassment with a smile.

Alex watched Raphael move off the wall. The movement caught Miguel's eye and he pivoted squarely to face Raphael.

"Hey, now we are all on the same team here," Alex cautioned. "I don't want an apocalyptic war to start in my quarters."

"I don't know whether we are all on the same team," Raphael placed emphasis on the word all, drawing scrutiny from everyone.

"The only being in this room that is questionable is you, Raphael. Tread with care," Alex cautioned knowing that all in the room had aligned themselves behind him and Miguel.

"Brother, you will see that it doesn't have to be this way," Miguel smiled. "What you saw and what you think you know may not be the direction that you believe will be taken."

"We will see, brother, and I pray that you are right. I have received no orders that will cause trouble as of yet. My orders thus far are to protect the Keeper and observe," Raphael leaned back against the wall with feigned indifference.

CHAPTER TWENTY-NINE

Alex was deep in conversation with Augy and Dr. Ferguson when the roaring and screeching started. He spun around to find Lina had shape-shifted into a red dragon. Gaseous fire exited her mouth like a giant flame thrower from the two valves in her large dragon head. The two harpies were deflecting the flames using their wings and magic. The raging fire spread quickly around the room.

The hungry flames licked and held onto the fabrics and rich tapestries that lined the walls and windows. The feminine touch that Lina applied to the apartment was going up in flames, which would set off the sprinklers alerting the human fire department.

Alex hopped over the back end of a couch to Lina. Using both hands, he managed to get the tip of her dragon snout closed and yelled to Sam and Max to extinguish the fire with magic. Augy and Doc used the fire extinguishers to tame the flames.

He turned towards the two harpie intruders and snarled, "You are uninvited."

Alex heard the hissing of gas and turned his head to find Lina's dragon form had grown another head. He raised a finger in warning to his wife.

Aello and Celano dropped their heads in apology. "We had an open invitation to the abode of the Nightwalker at one point in time."

Lina shifted back into human form; shoving Alex's hand aside, she snapped her fingers extinguishing the flames. "Exactly, That was history and when his home was not shared by me."

Alex knew Lina was pissed; her Spanish accent was evident whenever she got angry. Now it was so thick, he wondered if any of it was English.

"What happened to you was quite unfortunate," Celano began.

"Your father is very manipulative," Aello finished.

"Why are you here?" Alex asked circling his arm around Lina.

"We have some information," Celano began.

"That you may find helpful," Aello finished.

"Go on," Alex probed.

"Her father made a deal with an Underling harpie, giving her the ability to draw our strength. In one body, our combined strength is unmatchable by many," Celano began.

Alex remembered the power rippling off the harpie, Eataline. He wondered how she got the power, or the smarts to kill the harpie that made the deal with the devil. He looked to Aello for the next part of the story.

"That Underling walked terra and found a wet nurse for him. It was she who inspired the attack to bring down the archangel, and she who held the daemon prince," Aello continued.

Celano took up the next part of the story. "The Nightwalker was very clever to bring the grievances of the harpies to the Keeper, where the harpie driven by the darkness was stricken by the Angel of Light. If you had so harmed her yourself Nightwalker, she would have drawn your powers, too."

Aello blinked. "While this wet nurse's location is only known now to one, you would not be wise to seek it out."

"And why is that?" Alex scanned Aello's once more youthful face.

"Because, Nightwalker, only the fallen may enter," Celano finished.

"What do you want in return for this helpful information?" Alex asked.

"We realize that we are now in debt for two favors," Aello began.

"We wish to be released from one," Celano finished.

"Granted," Alex answered. "So where do we find the information we seek?"

"In the blood," The harpies answered in unison before dematerializing.

CHAPTER THIRTY

"What does that mean?" Lina asked pacing. "I can't take the riddles right now."

"What is fallen?" Sam asked

"Lina's father is a fallen angel," Raphael offered matter-of-factly.

"Why?" Sam pushed.

"Because he fell from grace," Raphael responded.

"So, then is Miguel also a fallen angel?"

Lina stared at Miguel, who approached filling out Alex's dress shirt in excess of the fabric's design. While he fitted into Alex's pants, the material stretched across him like a second skin. Nothing was left to the imagination.

"I am."

Lina could see the stony face Miguel wore, and knew his heart must be heavy to admit the lesser status.

"Miguel…" she began.

"It's okay. It is what it is. I am now amongst the fallen, therefore I can go and save the child," Miguel held up his hand before nodding to Lina and Alex. "I cannot seek out the blood. That, you must do alone."

Lina resumed her pacing. Her heart elated at the thought of her child. Her mind raced with possibilities. "Okay, Okay. Here is a plan. Alex and I will go below." She stared at Alex. "Amor I have an idea where my father keeps a hidden stash of blood with all his secret memories."

"Is that why I only find a little information or glimpses of information when I draw blood from him?" Alex queried.

"Yes, he hides his memories in pockets of blood hidden on the seventh level. This blood is locked away with old magic. I have an idea where it all is. I remember as a child being whipped to the bone for playing in an area designated as 'off limits.' Old habits die hard."

"So, we will go below to figure out the location. I can link that back to Jack," Alex mused.

"And I can tell Miguel," Jack finished.

"What should we do?" Sam asked holding onto Max.

"Perhaps you should deal with the authorities?" Augy suggested. I believe the fire alarm will have the fire department on the way."

"I don't want them in my quarters," Alex looked at Lina who nodded.

"Sam and Max, maybe you could stage the conference room down the hall to look like a fire? It's close enough to be here, right?" Lina asked.

"I'll go with them," Augy offered.

Lina nodded and he set off after Sam and Max.Grabbing Alex's hand, Lina burst out in a whirlwind descent to hell.

"Are you okay, my love?" Alex asked, trying to sway her curls to stay tucked behind her ears in the hurricane winds of hell's transport.

Lina took comfort in Alex's chest, after he snapped his wings open to shield them from the raging effects of the transport. "I'm a little scared."

Lina could see the surprise in Alex's face. She had surprised herself in admitting the emotion.

"Why?"

"Scared that we are too late, scared that this little life has been on its own this whole time and scare of failing it somehow." Lina looked upwards, her eyes brimming with blood tears.

"We will find him, or her, and there will be no failure." Alex's voice was gruff; Lina knew this to be an emotional sign.

She cleared her throat. "The transport will drop us off in the council chambers. I need to check there for a key. We'll have to be quick. He'll know you've arrived. He may not be sure about me. If he catches us in chambers, you'll have to stall him."

"Won't he see you? I'll mask myself, but you'll have to have a good story in case he back-drafts your blood and sees your memories."

"I'll be ready," Alex nodded. "And you?"

"I'll be careful," Lina smiled.

The transport dropped them in the center of council chambers. Alex jumped over the semicircular stone table. He sat in his seat heading the sixth level of hell and sank his talons into the chair not waiting for the chair's natural ability to replenish him. With his talons drawing the blood forth at an exponential rate, he searched hell's memories.

Lina knew her father would be alerted to Alex's arrival, but figured that it would also mask her activities, because Alex was parsing intense volumes of blood.

She gave a fleeting look towards him before letting him know that she'd found the key. He looked casual enough with his feet resting on the semicircular table top. Lina could barely see his talons sunk deep into the chair. Alex rested his head on the back. Lina knew he wasn't sleeping, but searching and waiting for her father. The best position with her father was not always an offensive one.

Returning to her mission, she scurried along the passage way, careful not to touch any of the prison bars that floated alongside the hallways. The cries of the banshees that were restrained within the hallways carried for miles, one screech from any one of them would send a message alerting her father of a presence. No one dared travel these hallways anymore.

Flames illuminated the hallways upon her approach, attempting misdirection at each turn. Lina ignored them charting her course from childhood memory. She heard her father roar in pain. Frozen in her tracks, she listened for any indicators, acknowledging that she couldn't turn back. If she had to hazard a guess, she'd bet that Alex was now drawing blood from him.

She set forward, a quick left and a right brought her to the forbidden garden. Slipping the key into the lock in the rock wall, Lina heard the grating of rock on rock as the door, invisible even to her own eyes, opened. Birds chirped pleasing melodies; butterflies frolicked among the flowers that laced the grass; and warm sunlight filter through the trees casting sugared patterns on the grassy rug. Lina levitated forward. She dare not touch the grass. Every aspect of the garden would alert her presence. The entire environment was a farce, a wrong step could get her and Alex killed.

She flitted from tree to tree like a magpie looking for a sign, a flicker of a memory. Nothing seemed familiar until she came to an old crab apple tree. Its bark was rough, ugly, and laden with lichen. The apples bruised and smelled strangely tart. Hesitantly placing her fingers above the largest bough, she extended her upper and lower fangs and closed her eyes moments before sinking her fangs into the tree, gripping it with her talons and holding on for dear life.

The garden began to dissolve. The roars of anger and pain became louder, growing like a philharmonic crescendo until they were so loud, they had to be real. Lina opened her eyes only to find her fangs sunk deep into her father's right shoulder. The crab apple tree bough had become his right arm.

She closed her eyes again, intensifying her grip, drawing harder upon the blood, searching for the single memory she needed. The flames in the chambers began to extinguish one by one. Lina felt Alex let go. She ravaged through the rest of the blood until she found what she was looking for.

Extracting her fangs, she gulped for air.

"Did you get it?" Alex asked between breaths. He was panting and gasping for breath himself.

"Si Amor, I got it." Lina got up, noticing one flame was left. She stared in disgust at the shriveled image of a man lying before her. His skin wrinkled in competition with dehydrated fruit. He no longer fit the arrogant air of a king of any dominion. She was half tempted to expire him for good.

"Then let's go," Alex got up.

Lina felt Alex's hand reaching for her, pulling her towards him. She stared at him. If she expired her father then Alex would have to assume the role of King of the Underworld. Neither of them wanted that punishment.

"Wait!" Lina wiped her mouth of the dark blood and flung the spittle filled substance at her father. "Here, use what you can to recover. This is more than you gave me. Just know there are some things you shouldn't fuck with."

She grabbed Alex's hand. As Alex's wings surrounded her, she sank her teeth into his neck and winced when she felt him sink his own into her. She sent him the mental image she stole from her father's memories and what she had learned of the location.

More so, she found the peace that steadied her and squelched the fury that rode just beneath her skin.

CHAPTER THIRTY-ONE

"Have you heard anything?"

"Patience," Miguel caught Jack mid pacing and stared into her eyes. "You are wearing a path into sub-terra with your pacing. Besides, you will get the message first."

"Right. Of course. I'm just worried for them." Jack wrung her hands. "I'm not used to being the one who gets left behind."

Miguel saw a strange look come over Jack. "You've heard?"

"Yes, they sent an image. I don't know how to send it to you?" she waved her hands.

Miguel smiled, seeing the frantic look in her eyes. He bent over and kissed her, sending calm energy, while he read her memories. "I'll be back," he whispered.

"How will you get there?"

Miguel smiled at her honest question seeing that she had made a small attempt at catering to his emotions by squinting her eyes.

"I can still use a rift even though I don't have my wings." He smiled again. "I'll be back."

Miguel landed on the white sand beach on the eastern shore of the island of Crete. "How appropriate," he muttered. He realized that the child was probably being kept in the cave of Crete, where Zeus had been hidden. He wondered if Alexander would appreciate the irony of this location. "How history repeats itself. I wonder if it was Cronus, who bespelled the cave, so only the fallen may enter after it was vacated."

The winds seemed to whisper to him as he walked along the sands. Alex's leather shoes were not the optimal footwear for walking in the sand, but Miguel didn't want to remove the footwear, rocks lay ahead. Making short bursts through a rift wouldn't get him any closer, besides using a lot of energy. Walking like a human would have to do.

I should watch my tongue, Miguel thought. *I recall history speaking of nymphs that lived here raising Zeus. I must have a care before they take hold of me and render me useless to the team.*

As he headed down the beach, he felt lulled by the wash of the clearest crystalline waters lapping against the shores. The breeze played with the leaves in the trees, making soft music. Miguel shook his head to clear his thoughts. He fixated on Jack, recalling her soft smooth skin and firm body. Her jade green eyes melting in the shadows of his brought a smile to his lips.

He began his ascent up the rock, focusing on the many faces of Jack. A frown passed his brows as he acknowledged the role that Raphael now played. A role, he vowed, that would be limited to that of a guardian. Raphael dare not step fully into his shoes.

Miguel made short work of scaling the remainder of the rocks to the mouth of the cave.

The wet nurse was a nymph. She taunted him in a high pitched sing-songy voice from the mouth of the cavern.

"Have a care beautiful angel. Have a care before you fall. The wet rocks are slippery. Though only the truly fallen may enter. Are you sure you want what you seek?"

Miguel walked into the mouth of the cave without issue, sending the nymph shrieking towards the rear of the cave. He could hear the baby crying. He shook his head, never imagining that he would have to chase a nymph to retrieve a child. Chasing nymphs never worked. They would lead the unsuspecting on a trail fashioned with glamour until you had forgotten your purpose. Every step into glamour weakened their victims until they awoke fully under the nymph's spell, where glamour was no longer necessary.

Walking towards the cries of the baby, Miguel settled hi in the middle of the cavern. Finding the smoothest rock, he lowered his body onto it until he could cross his legs. He felt the fabric of Alex's pants straining as his legs crossed. He decided that high fashion was not functional.

Closing his eyes, he began to pray, keeping his ears open should the nymph launch an attack.

The temperature in the cave dropped as the sun set. Miguel heard the rhythm of tiny footsteps echoing around the cave. A smiled played at the corner of his mouth. The little nymph had lasted. He could almost triangulate the position of her. When the footsteps stop, he leapt from his position. He landed on the nymph forty feet away, pinning her by her throat. Her aquamarine blue eyes blazed with fury. Each one of her sharp fanged teeth gnashed, ready to rip his flesh given the chance. She was beautiful, although her tattered seaweed coverings gave away her age. Her wings sparkled like the ocean on a moonlit night. Miguel considered ending the creature's miserable life; her eyes emitted certain sadness and despair.

"I'm going to let you go," said he told her.

She looked confused. He relaxed his hand when she stopped gnashing her teeth.

"I'm going to let you go. Do you understand me?" Miguel raised an eyebrow.

The nymph nodded. "You do not wish to kill me?"

"No," Miguel shook his head. "I have only come for the child."

"Most would want me to grant them wishes. You do not plan to use me?" The nymph narrowed her beguiling eyes.

Miguel let her go as he stated he would. He was surprised when she began to laugh at him.

"How will you leave?" she asked. "Only the fallen may enter and only the saved may leave. Even I am stuck here. I have been trapped here since Cronus placed his spell on the cave. To see the water I crave so fiercely and yet not be able to swim in it, or touch only what has pooled in the lower caves from high tide. Mayhaps it would be better if you kill me."

"Were you the only one trapped?"

"No," the nymph sighed. "There were others. We were the ones who cared for Zeus. Being trapped here for an eternity was our punishment. I had nothing left until he gave me this new child to care for, and now you would take that away? I cannot spend another eternity with no more than these same old withering rocks. Even they fade with age."

"How does he leave?" Miguel asked looking around the cave for traces of an exit.

"There is a gateway beyond that goes down below, but even he cannot go out the same way he comes in. That is where the others went. They wanted to go anywhere but stay here. They perished. We aren't meant to live down there. We were of the water, not fire."

"Please give me the child."

"What about me?" she asked. "I have never asked anything of anyone as I ask now. Will you take me, too?"

"I will try to get us all out; I cannot promise anything. I have faith that we will all be fine; the truth is, if I'm wrong, we may all die this very day."

"You are honest at least. I will take that over anything. So many years have passed. To perish may be better than suffering for another eternity."

Miguel waited as the nymph retrieved the child. She flitted over the larger boulders and jumped from rock to rock. Little giggles of mirth brought smiles to her face as she bounced down from the heights of the cave to where he waited. He stared at the swaddled mass thrust upwards into his hands. A crest of dark brown curls breached the blankets.

Miguel looked down at the nymph's expectant face. "Let's go."

He walked to the cave's mouth with the baby cradled in one hand and the nymph's hand in his other. Closing his eyes he smiled. The nymph's voice played in the breeze, "Thank you beautiful angel, I will never forget you."

CHAPTER THIRTY-TWO

"What's going on here?" Alex asked with Lina in tow. Sam, Max, and Jack were standing in the hallway in front of the conference room doors. Firefighters milled about and a familiar face was directing traffic.

"I just asked the same question." Jack looked at Sam.

"I thought they would be gone by now," Alex looked around.

"It's all my fault," Sam whispered.

"Well not really; I don't think we are the best at creating a scene, so to speak," Max shook his head.

"What happened?" Alex drew them closer.

"Well, we got this idea that something needed to start the fire, so we put one of Max's digital things on the conference room table and brought a glass of water. The idea was to say the glass spilled onto the electronics and started an electrical fire. I quickly scorched the room and wet the room including us. We swapped the fire extinguishers and sprayed some more and thought we did a good job." "Except that the fire fighters came in and said it was curious the path the fire took, because fire doesn't usually travel the way it appears to have traveled. Apart from the fire's signature... they said that some of the stuff we brought from the other room and the stuff already in the conference room don't look like they were in the same fire." Max chimed in lowering his voice. "Apparently they can tell that one looks like a gas fire and the other some other kind of fire."

"And the sprinklers don't appear to have ever been used. Apparently, there was some paper hanging from the ceiling tile that never got wet. Left over from an office party, perhaps?" Sam went on.

Alex watched as Lina peeked inside the room. She snapped her fingers. Shouts and screams could be heard from within the conference room.

Alex raised his eyebrows.

Lina shrugged her shoulders, "I just wanted them to know that the sprinklers worked. And perhaps create a few other things that are unexplainable in their presence. I have found when they witness the unexplainable themselves, they are more likely to come up with an explanation that they feel will suit the occasion just so they don't have to really deal with it."

Alex chuckled.

"Ah, everyone is here."

Alex spun around at the sound of the unwelcome, but familiar voice. "Detective, how good to see you again. It's been a while now."

Alex stuck out his hand to Ed Trattoria.

"Eh," Trattoria grabbed Alex's hand, pumping it up and down furiously. "Xander Macedo. Didn't we just see each other the other day? What was it an infrastructure glitch I believe you said?"

"Not that I can recall. I don't have anything to do with the building affairs." Alex said thoughtfully, wondering if he had played himself or Lex Macedo at their last meeting. "Perhaps you met my brother, Lex? It's his company. Some say we look alike; he's a little broader and taller, but with facial hair."

"Hmm," Ed Trattoria smoothed back his wet hair. "Perhaps."

Another series of shouts from the conference room erupted in cheers. Alex peeked in with anticipated curiosity. The fire fighters had figured out how to turn the sprinklers off. "So it is strange that a detective has responded to a fire call? Should I be worried?" Alex asked.

"There have been a number of calls to the tower recently. So a detective is sent to assure no foul play. It's just procedure. You know."

Ed Trattoria's Staten Island accent was thick and his mannerisms that accompanied it got under Alex's skin. "I think I'll contact my brother anyway, if you suspect foul play, he should be aware." Alex feigned a serious tone. "So you say this is not a normal fire," he raised his eyebrows.

Ed Trattoria sighed. "Not that it isn't normal, we just have to check it out."

"Oh, so it is normal. Good." He circled his arm around Lina's waist. "Then you'll be off Detective. Thank you for being the one to personally handle the investigation."

"Yes, just a few things to wrap up here. I'll let you get back to getting dressed as it seems you were interrupted."

Alex looked down, realizing that he still hadn't put on a shirt since he had relinquished it to Lina and she was still dressed in her dragon skin dress. Alex leaned forward.

"Actually Detective, it was the other way around. My wife and I were just getting out of our clothes when we got here and realized the commotion."

Alex watched Lina give Ed a huge smile winking at him for good measure.

"Ah, Mrs. Macedo," Ed Trattoria glanced at Max. "Max's step-mother. I'm putting it all together now." He stuffed his documents under his arm and pointed his forefingers at them. "Last time we met you were pregnant. Congratulations are in order I suppose."

Alex glanced at Lina hearing the boom from a rift slapping closed. "The baby."

Extending his hand to the Detective, Alex smiled. "Yes, thank you, Detective. Again, I'm glad you are here to keep things in order." He turned to Max his smile fading only slightly. "Have B. meet you here and wrap things up with the good Detective, then join us."

Max nodded.

Alex set off briskly down the hallway with his entourage following closely behind.

CHAPTER THIRTY-THREE

Alex was first through the door to his condominium. "What in any name is going on?" he demanded.

Miguel stood holding a blanketed bundle with his palm extended towards Raphael, who maintained an offensive pose with his sword drawn.

"Sam, a sound block please," Alex barked as he strode over to Miguel to take the baby.

He felt the wave of magic ride over him as Sam magically provided a sound barrier.

Alex peaked at the little bundle, below the barrage of curls, lay a peaceful sleeping face. He kissed the sleeping baby boy's forehead before passing him to the anxious nearly impatient Lina. He gave her a reassuring smile.

"Raphael, why is your sword drawn? There will be no bloodshed in this house. Our family has been made whole, we will be rejoicing tonight. Join us, brother."

Raphael gave Alex a look and withdrew his sword. Alex nodded his head in return to Raphael's bow, and shrugged his shoulders at Miguel when the angel disappeared.

"Mig, I don't know how you pulled this off, but thank you." Alex pulled him into a full embrace. To his surprise the usually angry angel beamed him a smile.

"You are welcome Alexander. Quite welcome."

"So what was all that about with the healer?"

"I asked him to step down as Jack's Light Warrior. He refused, saying he has received no orders that change his current command."

"Hmpf, so I guess we'll be stuck with him for a bit then. What about you? I take it you got your colors back?"

Miguel grinned from ear to ear. "I did."

"Let's see then? I always like to make sure I recognize you." Alex laughed.

Miguel unbuttoned Alex's shirt, removing it, he snapped his wings open. Platinum blue angel dust flew everywhere, drawing shrieks from the ladies.

"Amor, Miguel, no angel dust in the house, please. I'm allergic, and we don't know if the baby is, too."

"Sorry," Alex grinned. To say Lina was allergic was an understatement. As a daemon, angel dust was quite painful. It didn't bother Alex. He wondered if the baby were more daemon, or more vampire. "You pretty much got your same colors back. Except, there's a little more going on at the base of the wings?" Alex remarked.

"I will admit that I was a little concerned about them. I don't want to seem like I'm obsessed or anything," Miguel grinned.

"It's okay to take stock in your appearance," Alex grinned.

"So what are you going to call the baby?" Miguel laughed closing his wings and putting back on Alex's shirt.

"You know Mig; we have spent so much time chasing down the whereabouts of everyone in this room, that we have nothing ready. We haven't thought about baby names or anything, at least any that we've discussed." Alex reached into his phone and requested one of his staff to go shopping for the basics for a baby boy. Closing the phone, he looked back at Miguel, "So, with Raphael still in the picture as Jack's guardian, what will you be doing?"

Miguel shook his head. "I've been reinstated as a Warrior of the Light, but I have no orders as of yet. I think I'll get to know Jack a little better and see what happens. I'm sure something will. There's never a dull moment with you guys."

Alex watched Miguel fiddle with his hands.

"I do have something to take care of though. If Jack asks, tell her I'll be back."

"Okay, everything alright? I'm a good wing man if you need one."

"Not this time, brother."

"Come back in one piece," Alex smiled. "I don't want to have to do any explaining." He nodded in Jack's direction.

Alex felt Miguel's hand restraining him. He had presumed the angel would have just left after his last comment. After casting a quick glance at the restraining hand, he asked, "What's up?"

"I guess I haven't asked you how you feel about Jack and me."

Alex chuckled. "Seems like a popular question. I'm glad she's happy Mig. Honest I am. I have deep feelings for her, but there's something about her that prohibits me from crossing that line. Respect for her at best. If she's happy with you, then I'm happy, too. I hope that's good enough, I don't have much more of an explanation."

Alex averted his gaze to the ladies still fawning over the new baby. He realized that post explanation, Miguel had left.

Smiling, he walked over to see what they were fussing about. As he got closer, he could hear the little gurgles of delight which changed his smile to a grin.

CHAPTER THIRTY-FOUR

Miguel landed on the observation deck of the Sears tower. He tugged at the bottom of his jacket, a small pleasure to be back in the comfort of his own clothing. Flexing his muscles into the very familiar cut of his suit, he exhaled, reaching a level of calm that he was looking for.

His stride seemed effortless. He walked around the antennae structures towards the crumpled shell of a man seated with his legs crossed on a parapet overlooking Chicago. The man could have been sitting on a park bench with the ease that he portrayed. Instead, being a good near two thousand feet above sea level, he swayed occasionally when the breezes toyed with him.

"You won't change anything if you kill me."

Miguel's face regained the stony mask of the angry angel he usually portrayed, as he regarded the rear silhouette of the man. "You presume that I would kill you."

"If you did, he'd just become what I am. Your efforts would be futile. Essentially, I would become him. That destiny is in the blood."

"His fate," Miguel laughed, "does not lie with you. He charts his own course."

"As we all do to some degree. Why have you come? To banter with an old man?"

"You are far from being an old man, Lucifer." Miguel spat the daemon king's name out as Lucifer swiveled around to face him.

"Semantics," he shrugged his shoulders.

"Your façade doesn't evoke any sympathy from me," Miguel regarded him. He really did look like a frail old man. His skin was translucent and hung limply from his skeleton. Blue pulsing veins bobbed at his temples. Dark rings shadowed his sunken brown eyes. No power rippled off this once formidable opponent, all he was missing to complete the façade was a walking frame. Miguel sneered, even his clothing hung strangely over the misshapen body. He wondered what Alex and Lina had done to cause the grandeur and arrogance to depart the daemon king, who had once taken the form of a ten horned red dragon to fight him. Now he didn't appear to have the energy to take any form, but the fragile shell he maintained now.

"This is no façade," Lucifer hung his head. "Perhaps you should kill me while you can," a feeble smile cracked Lucifer's face, revealing yellow stained teeth.

Miguel lunged forward, drawing his sword and pointing it at Lucifer's throat. He allowed the tip of the blade to draw blood. "I have the child."

Lucifer's eyes open in surprise. "Is that so?"

"It is."

"Don't you feel played?"

"It won't be the first time. There'll be other opportunities. We are each pawns in someone's game, Miguel pointed out."

The smile returned to Lucifer's face and Miguel tried not to empathize with him. His own faith had waivered when he felt forsaken. "Should this blade remove your head, I'll know you can never bring him harm or undue influence."

"If it's not me, it'll be someone else. Better the devil you know. No?" Lucifer's voice broke with the pressure of the sword against his larynx.

Lightning crackled, hitting one of the antennae topping the skyscraper.

Miguel's smile could not be mistaken for kind in any light. He withdrew his sword. "I guess both the fallen have been saved this day. Another day will come." Miguel's seething voice faded on the Chicago breezes.

EPILOGUE

Detective Ed Trattoria pored over the case files littered over his desk. The florescent overhead light flickered to an annoying rhythm that toyed with his concentration. He pushed his left eyebrow further into his forehead, as he attempted to wipe the distraction from his mind.

He scribbled furiously on the yellow sticky squares he adorned the case files with, rummaging through them to validate his thoughts.

Trattoria was so engrossed; he didn't hear the approaching footsteps.

"Oh," Louis stuck his head through the door and said.

"Holy shit Lou," Trattoria swung back in his desk chair. "What?"

"You scared the shit out of me," Trattoria wiped the sweat off of his brow. "What'd I tell you about sneaking up on me like that?"

"Dude, I just walked 'ere. C'mon! I'ma big fella 'ere, I sure didn't tippy toe," Louis shook his head, his Staten Island accent just as thick as Trattoria's.

"So whatdya want?" Trattoria leaned back in the chair.

"Some of the boys are going to meet up at Joe's. You wanna come?"

Trattoria eyeballed the sealed brown envelope that Louis was waving around as he spoke. "Nah, I got some stuff here that I wanna go through one last time."

"Eddy," every time there's a call for that Macedo building you open that file and spend days at it; you find nothing but loose ends. Leave it alone. That guy must donate millions of dollars to the city, and has never been linked to not so much as an unpaid parking ticket, let alone whatever it is you are trying to find."

Trattoria sighed as he watched the envelope. "Whatcha got there?" He motioned to Louis to hand it over.

"Yeah some guy dropped it off and said to give it to you. Don't stay up 'ere long. You'll go blind. We'll be at Joe's."

"Yea. Yea." Trattoria waved him off and stared at packet for about five minutes. No writing adorned the outside of the 9 x 12 nondescript envelope. The only thing special about it was the care that someone had gone to, to make sure that no immediately identifiable marks were left on it.

Smiling, Trattoria vowed to send the envelope to forensics to check out the glue seal, just in case the sender had used saliva to seal it. He banged the envelope on the table to drop the contents to the other side. Reaching into his pants pocket, he took out his penknife. Carefully breaking the seal, he raised the envelope and let the contents slide out onto his desk.

White papers slid out, their order retained by a large binder clip. Trattoria eyed the clip for fingerprints; none were visible to the naked eye. The one thing that jumped out at him was the name printed boldly on the front of the papers. "Leonides"

****

Alex crept into bed. His hand found the round of Lina's buttocks. He smiled; she giggled.

"Come here woman. This has been a long day," he sighed, feeling exhausted but finding the energy to reach for her naked body. He could do with another pack of bank blood, or even one of Sam's bottles of La Sangre de Vida; he was too tired to get up.

He smoothed Lina's tresses as she curled up in his arms. "You feel so good," he whispered. "Is the baby asleep?"

"Yes, Amor, you know we really have to think of a name before he grows up being called, Baby."

"Hmm, I'll get right on that." He planted kisses over her forehead and eyes. One hand reached for her full bottom while the other hand found her ripe breasts.

"Alejandro, I'm serious," Lina feigned seriousness as she arched her back. A soft moan escaped her lips

"Perhaps we'll settle on something before Baby gets a brother or sister," Alex responded between mouthfuls as he suckled Lina's breasts, "and then we'll have to call that one brother or sister."

A soft moan escaped her lips as she arched her back offering her breasts to him. Alex pulled her in close, repositioning her to be underneath him. His fangs dropped, as hunger gnawed at him, the hunger of desire and passion.

The ringing of Alex's mobile phone intruded upon the ambiance, followed by a high pitched wailing from the baby's crib.

"Ugh," he sighed as he rolled off Lina grappling for his mobile phone. He felt the bounce of the bed, and heard the scurry of footsteps as Lina ran to the baby's crib.

"Hello, hello," Alex said as he stuck his finger in his other ear to eliminate the cries. "Hello," he repeated, thankful that Lina was able to quiet the baby.

"Alexander, we have a problem."

Alex froze as his memory recollected the cadence of the voice over the distortion and static on the line. "Leonides?" His eyes caught the edge of a well crumpled paper sticking out of his pants pocket. He delved into it extracting the crumpled note that he had been meaning to read. The same note that he had taken from Blondie during the first attack.

He unfolded the note 'We know about Leonides' were the only words printed on the note. He flipped the paper over to be sure there were no other words or inscriptions that could be of consequence. Alex heard his name being called with increasing urgency over the phone. "Yes I'm here," he muttered as he placed the phone back at his ear.

"They know."

"Are you safe?"

"For now."

"We'll make arrangements. I'll be in touch!" Alex ended the call turning the meet Lina's worried gaze.

ABOUT THE AUTHOR

Bitten Twice is an author who primarily writes in the paranormal romance and urban fantasy genres. She released the first in the Macedo Ink vampire series in October of 2010.

Bitten Twice currently lives in Hollywood, FL with her family. Courageously in love with one man and two children, together they care for the family's two dogs. Bitten is a lifetime member of the Florida Writer's Association and an associate member of International Thriller Writers.

You can follow Bitten on the web:

Facebook: BittenTwice

Twitter: @bitten2ice

The Web: http://www.bitten2ice.com